Chapman Hall

Julie Fontenot Landry

Cover: Cat Landry Design
Cover Photo: Michael Landry
Photo used with permission of
Bolling Hall Museum, Bradford, UK

For Michael, who helped me to create this story
and without whose love and support this book
would never have become a reality.

Contents

Part I

Andrew Selden galloped down the country road, his long, tawny hair blending with the horse's mane as he leaned close to the animal's neck to dodge the low-hanging tree branches that his father's peasants had neglected to trim. The weather had been dry, and Sterling's hooves clattered and kicked up a swirl of dust instead of thudding cleanly on the normally spongy earth.

Soon the trees cleared, and he reined his mount before a neatly kept cottage, tying the sweating stallion to a rough-hewn hitching post just below one thatched gable.

At once a shutter in the gable creaked open noisily, and a woman's head popped out of the glassless window.

"She's in the barn, but don't be long about ye. She has her chores to do, ye know." Then blue eyes, rosy, round cheeks, and bonnet disappeared.

"No chores for Lucy today," Andrew mumbled in the general direction of the empty window. "Today I'm her only task." With that he took off full tilt for the barn behind the house, scattering chickens and geese in all directions.

The barn was dim, lit only by what light entered through the open doors at either end. All the barn's usual denizens were out to pasture for the day, and the only sound was the buzz of a handful of flies around a single pile of excrement not yet hauled away to the manure heap. Andrew made a cursory search of the stalls, then climbed the ladder to the loft.

"Lucy?" he called, but no answer came. Maybe her mother had been mistaken and she had gone out to the field. Then suddenly he felt arms around him from behind, and whirled.

"God's blood, you wench! You gave me a fright," he said, pulling her to him, marveling, as always, at her astonishing beauty. Her hair was the color of palest honey, her skin as smooth as that of a perfect peach, and of almost the same hue. A jewel fit for a king's crown, yet the daughter of a peasant! How was it possible?

But no eighteen-year-old in love will waste many moments in

1

abstract consideration of his beloved's lineage. Before his thoughts had time to form, the two of them were in the hay, devouring each other like starving beggars at a feast.

When they had had their fill of love, they lay in each other's arms. Lucy spoke first. "Andrew, love," she said.

Andrew, sluggish from his exertions and wanting a nap more than anything, merely grunted.

"Andrew, love," she said again. "Wake up. We must speak together."

Andrew managed to raise himself on one elbow. "What is it, my pretty wench?" he teased her. "You want me to ride to Shrewsbury and buy a ribbon at the market, is that it?" He leaned over and kissed her neck, still bare, and her right nipple, erect and pimply from the coolness creeping back into her resting body.

"No, Andrew. I wish that were all. It's much more than that I want," she said, her voice quivering and a tear starting from the corner of her eye.

Andrew pulled up, alarmed. Besides being beautiful, Lucy was perennially cheerful. He had known her since they were children, and he had never seen her weep, except once when she fell over a plow and cut a huge gash in her shin. She was always smiling and laughing, never petulant and nagging like most of the girls he knew.

"What is it, love?" he whispered, smoothing her hair back from her forehead.

"Andrew, I'm with child!" she wailed, dissolving into tears and sobbing against his chest.'"

"Father, I must speak with you!" Andrew's breathless words shot from his mouth as he burst into his father's closet. Thomas, Lord Selden, looked up at his son from the book he was reading, his visage as immobile as his son's was gorged with emotion.

"Andrew, I do not appreciate your not knocking before you enter. It shows want of breeding, and that is absurd in your case."

Andrew, apparently oblivious to his father's annoyance, barely paused long enough for the older man to finish his sentence.

"Father," he said, shutting the door noisily, "Lucy is with child!"

"Lucy who?" Lord Selden inquired without interest, bending his bald head over his book again.

"Lucy who? Why, Lucy Digby, of course, Father! What other Lucy is there in the world?"

"Lucy Digby? You mean Philip Digby's oldest girl? The one you used to play with when you were small?"

"Yes, Father, of course!"

"Well, so she's with child. That's her father's affair, not mine. I don't control my peasants' lives that thoroughly, though perhaps sometimes I should. Or has she married yet? No, I don't recall giving consent to the banns."

"No, she's not married, but I mean her to be soon."

"Oh, and when did you start taking an interest in the welfare of my peasants? I thought the army was all that occupied your mind. 'I'll not be a country bumpkin, not I,' say you often enough. 'I'll not have the court laugh at my backward ways.' And now you've decided to play the country gentleman. What will you do, give her part of your allowance for a dowry? God knows Philip was never frugal enough to have saved any, procreating like a rabbit as he does!"

Lord Selden glanced quickly at his son, knowing the patronizing would antagonize him, but not being able to resist the well deserved gibe. The boy was entirely too critical of his rural neighbors.

However, though the father expected a reaction, he did not expect the red face, narrowed eyes, and clenched teeth and fists he saw before him. As his eyes met his son's, Andrew took a step toward him, and Lord Selden recoiled instinctively.

"I don't give a damn about being a country gentleman! I think they are all as dull as the pigs in their pens. But when I become the father of a child, I want it to be cared for!"

"You? You sired a child on Philip Digby's girl? Bravo! Bravo! And you but how old? Eighteen isn't it? Well, I sired my first at fifteen, but eighteen isn't bad! Bravo, Son!"

His father's congratulations almost caused Andrew's fierce expression to abate, but then,

"Father, don't talk about her as if she were an animal!"

"Well, why not, for Christ's bones' sake? She's but a peasant, Boy! But if you're fond of the wench, I'll make her a nice match, say with one of Oliver Boyle's boys. I hear she's quite a beauty. And I'll give her a nice purse so that even Oliver, with his snooty bailiff's airs, won't balk. Will that do?"

Andrew leaned over his father trembling, shaking his fist in the older man's face. "How dare you speak of her like that! You will give her to no one. She is mine! And the child is mine!"

"Andrew, get a hold of yourself!" Lord Selden exclaimed, rising to his feet, grabbing his son's forearm, and pushing him backward. "I'll not have you shaking your fist at me. I don't know where you get your grand airs, but if it's so important to you, find a husband for her yourself, and pay him too!" He flung his book onto the table and started for the door.

"I have found her a husband," Andrew said to his back.

"Oh, really," said Lord Selden, turning around again. "Who?"

"The only person fit to raise my child."

"And who might that paragon of virtue be, prithee?"

"Myself."

"Yourself?" The whiteness of Lord Selden's face bore witness to the fact that he knew better than to think his son was joking. "Are you mad, Boy? The girl's a peasant, by God, a peasant! You are to be Andrew, Lord Selden, tenth earl of Wilmot!"

"Then I should have the power to give her father a barony," Andrew said smugly, "and she would no longer be a peasant but a noblewoman, a baron's daughter."

"So you've got it all figured out, have you? Andrew, this is folly! Philip Digby is a good man, but a baron! Why—why am I even discussing this with you? It's out of the question. Your grandfather would turn over in his grave."

"My grandfather is as dead as a stuffed grouse, and so shall you be when I do it, unless you listen to reason and do it for me now."

Lord Selden reddened from his short, stout neck over his hairless pate, and his broad chest heaved with emotion. "You shall not have her, I say; you shall not! I would have set her up for you as a mistress gladly, but to even suggest such a thing as marriage! I'll see you dead first!" He strode from the room, slamming the door behind him and bringing Oliver Boyle, his bailiff, out of the kitchen to the foot of the stairs to see what all the fuss was about.

Seeing Oliver's questioning look, Lord Selden motioned to him, and the two men walked in silence out of the house and into the dovecote on its left flank.

With the violence of his motion sending the birds flying through every aperture, Lord Selden paced the floor of the tiny stone building, Oliver Boyle leaning black-clothed against the door, his heavily browed face impassive as usual. "I want you to follow Andrew," Lord Selden said. "He will be heading for Philip Digby's place. Find out what plans he makes with Philip's oldest girl. Beat it out of her if you have to, but find out."

Boyle nodded almost imperceptibly, pulled his hat down even further over his brow, and walked away, leaving Lord Selden raging among the dove roosts.

Shortly a stallion hurtled out of the stableyard. Behind it, but out of eye- and ear-shot, a black-clothed rider followed, ambling slowly on a roan mare.

In the pink light of early morning a wagon could be seen driving away from the Digby cottage. It was piled high with furnishings, and cages of poultry hung from its sides. The stocky figure of a cow was tethered behind it, and the wagon moved slowly, at the cow's pace. Several human silhouettes were discernible on the bench and in the rear.

A single horseman accompanied the wagon, his face dark and

hooded in the shadowed dawn. The wagon clattered eastward and disappeared into the sun's rays on the horizon.

When Andrew arrived at the cottage two hours later, saddlebags packed for a journey, he found the homestead deserted. The cottage was tightly closed, the shutters unseasonably fastened. No smoke rose from the chimney; no chickens pecked about in the grass.

Frantic, Andrew flew to the barn, only to find its condition the same. The whole place had the stillness of death, or of the quiet that precedes a storm.

As his face blanched and sweat broke through his pores, Andrew bounded back to his thoroughly startled mount, dug in his heels, and sped back down the road the way he had come.

His parents were just sitting down to breakfast when Andrew stormed through the door and crashed his fist onto the table, upsetting a porcelain pitcher of cream and scattering plump, red strawberries all over the floor.

"What have you done with her?" he shouted, less that a foot from his father's ear.

"Andrew!" his father shouted back, standing to avoid the cream, which was on its way to his lap. "What do you mean coming in here like this and behaving like a barbarian?"

"Andrew, dear, this is shocking!" his mother interjected. "What if we'd had guests?"

"Old man, what have you done with her?" he asked again, through clenched teeth, his fingers tightly gripping his father's shirtfront.

"Andrew!" his mother screamed.

Then her scream faded from Andrew's consciousness as the force of Lord Selden's blow to his chin sent him flying across the room and against the seat beneath the bay window.

When Andrew awoke, he was in his own bed, and 'Lisbeth, the

old Welsh woman who had nursed him from babyhood, was standing over him. "Master Andrew? Master Andrew? Canst waken? Say thou canst, Sir!"

Andrew opened his eyes wide enough for her to see that he was awake. "'Lisbeth, what happened? Where am I?" His eyes found familiar objects then the canopy over the bed, the paned window, the privy chair. "Oh. But what am I doing in bed?" He began to pick his head up off the bolster. "God's blood! What's happened to my head?"

"Oh, Sir, your father, Sir!" The old woman twisted the damp towel she had in her hands and looked miserable.

"What? Has something happened to my father?" Andrew tried to rise again, but his head hurt too badly.

"No, Sir, nothing's happened to him, Sir. It was him what bumped you, Sir. Oh, my, and look at your poor head, Sir, swole up like to a summer melon." She leaned over him, trying to smooth down his long hair, all matted from the pillow.

Then his eyes settled on the saddlebags, lumped in the corner of the room, and he remembered, and the anger and frustration and his longing for Lucy shut out the pain in his head.

"'Lisbeth," he said, his voice barely a whisper, "what did he do with her? Where did he send her?"

"Oh, Master Andrew," the old woman wailed, "to be sure I don't know, really I don't. 'Tis rumored he sent Oliver Boyle, cursed be his black soul, to take poor Philip and all his family far away, no one knows where. Mary White, what lived hard by to them, said poor Polly was nigh to bursting with grief at leaving that place, where all her young ones was born. Said it would have broke your heart to see her. And all the wee ones bawling along with her."

"Did Lucy go with them?"

"Aye, that she did, though Mary said she never shed a tear, not even when Philip beat her within an inch of her life."

"He beat her?" Andrew sprang to a sitting position, ignoring the pain that splintered his skull, but having to fall back down as the lack of blood to his brain sent the room spinning. "That bastard! Peasant scum! Doesn't he know she's with child?"

"Aye, Sir, he does, and it goes ill with him too, I hear. Mary heard him say he hoped it died, and Lucy along with it."

"I'll kill him," Andrew yelled, flailing back and forth with his head on the bolster and beating his fists against the counterpane. "As God is my witness, I'll kill him!"

"Master Andrew, you must stay quiet. You can't do yourself or Lucy or your child any good as you are. You must get well first. Your old noggin has had a bad blow."

"All right, 'Lisbeth, I'll be still, but not for long. Do whatever you have to, to make this damned head right again. I don't care if you have to get a spell from the devil himself."

The old woman winced at his reference to her reputed trafficking in witchcraft. She knew, as he did, that only his father's enlightened refusal to believe that such things as witches and devils existed had kept the old woman from being burned at the stake. In no other house in the county would she have been kept, especially not as a trusted servant. "Ah, Master Andrew," she said, "you know I've no such thing. Many's the time ye've been to the wood with me. Ye know what's my 'spells.' 'Tis naught but the leaves of the trees and the petals of flowers, all God's good creatures, what I use to make people well."

"Yes, 'Lisbeth, I know that," Andrew muttered impatiently. "Just get a move about you and get some of them so I can get out of this bed. I've got to find Lucy before that madman of a father of hers kills her and my child or before my equally mad father marries her off to some rustic oaf."

"All in good time, Master Andrew, all in good time," the old woman chuckled. "Thou wast always in a hurry, Sir, even as a little tyke."

As the old woman left the room, still enjoying her memories of a younger and more tractable Andrew, the object of her consideration closed his eyes and began to search his pain-dulled brain for ideas of where his father might have resettled the Digbys. Surely he would keep Philip; the man was his best mower, wielding the scythe like five men at once. Andrew had often seen the muscles ripple across Philip's back, even under his homespun shirt, as he leveled a stand of wheat. When he thought of those same muscles wielding whatever he had used to beat Lucy, his anger drove all rational thought from his head and only with difficulty did he calm himself enough to continue to think and plan.

He would make a systematic investigation, starting with Oliver Boyle. If Boyle—whom Andrew knew to be completely loyal to his father, even to the point of criminality—if Boyle wouldn't tell him, he'd go from manor to manor until he found her and brought her back and married her. If his father disinherited him, he'd get money from his maternal grandfather and go to America. In London he had met that fellow John Smith, a commoner to be sure, but by all accounts a gentleman and a brave man, and Smith had told him there was a fine life to be led in America, a life free of English snobbery, where a man could choose for himself and where Lucy, with her peasant skills, would be an asset rather than a liability. Andrew had never been close to his mother or her family, but it was worth a try.

Despite the ministrations of 'Lisbeth, who poulticed and dosed him with multicolored substances both sweet and bitter, mild and caustic, Andrew was bedridden for a week. Even after he was up and around, his head still ached every time he moved it any other way except gingerly, his impatience to be off on his search for Lucy checked daily by pain.

He had resolved to beat his father at his own game. During his time in bed, he realized that he had been entirely too open, that he should have known his father would never agree to his marrying a peasant, that he should have found some avaricious priest, God knew there were enough of those, who would marry them without publishing the banns. He had even seen a play at one of the London theaters about an Italian couple who had done just that. They had come to a bad end, true, but that was just a play, and Will Shakespeare, the playwright, was known to have a flair for the tragic.

So on the rare occasions when his father came in to see how he was doing, he said nothing about Lucy. His father never referred to her either, or even to the blow that had incapacitated his son, much less to the fact that it was he who had administered the blow. They talked only about safe things, his plans to outfit a regiment in the spring, his father's concerns as justice of peace and as member of the House of Lords. His father invited Andrew to join him in London when Parliament's fall session opened, and he agreed as if nothing had happened between them.

But as soon as his head was really healed, he cornered Oliver Boyle, having already determined from 'Lisbeth that none of Oliver's sons had married Lucy. He found Boyle at the kennel, working with his father's hunting hounds.

"Ho, Oliver," he said, slapping the older man on the back in false camaraderie, "are we likely to have good hunting this fall? Will the dogs be at their best, do you think?"

"Aye, Sir, I think so," said the older man warily, shutting the last yelping dog into its cage. Even in the summer heat Oliver never removed his black wool coat, and the sweat poured down his forehead. He cocked his left eyebrow upward and looked at Andrew as if expecting more conversation, but he spoke no more himself. From numerous dealings with the man, Andrew had noticed that Oliver never initiated statements; he only replied to questions, taking his cue from the tone of the questioner, if that questioner was his better.

"And have you been out in the field lately? Have you seen game about?"

"Aye, Sir, that I have," Oliver replied.

"Well, what did you see?" Andrew asked.

"What did I see, Sir?" Oliver repeated, as if he hadn't understood the question.

This man is infuriating, thought Andrew. He will not tell me a thing until he knows exactly what I want to hear.

"Yes, Oliver, did you see any pheasants?" He knew good and well Oliver hadn't seen any pheasants this early.

"No, Sir, I did not."

Well, thought Andrew, at least we're getting somewhere.

"Then what's the news hereabouts? You know I've been ill, and 'Lisbeth tells me only gossip."

"Thou'rt wise not to listen to old women, Sir," Oliver chortled through his broken and blackened teeth.

Oh, this one knows his lessons well, thought Andrew. Do exactly what the master wants. Laugh on cue, answer on demand.

"But she tells me that Philip Digby and his family have moved away. Is that true?" Andrew asked, as nonchalantly as possible.

"'Tis true Philip's cottage is empty, Sir," Oliver said, his face unreadable.

"You know where they are, don't you, Oliver?" Andrew was tired of the game. He wanted some answers. "In fact, it was you who took them away."

"That's as it may be, Sir," said Oliver, his eye contact with Andrew never flinching.

"Oliver, I demand that you tell me!" Andrew was red in the face now, his knuckles white as he clutched his riding crop.

"I am but a servant, Sir," Oliver replied, his tones honeyed and conciliating. "I do what I'm told. As for what I'm told to do, that you'll have to ask your father."

"I can see that I'm getting nowhere with you, Oliver, but just remember, my father will not live forever. In a few years I will be master here, and you will still be a young man. Think carefully before you cross me."

"Aye, Sir, that I do," Oliver replied, a hint of the facetious in his voice. With that he walked away toward the barn, leaving Andrew stewing.

That condescending bastard, Andrew cursed inwardly. I'll cut that insolent tongue out of his mouth one day.

But he knew it was hopeless to spend any more time with Boyle. He was Lord Selden's creature, more devoted than any dog.

So Andrew spent the next two weeks on horseback scouring the countryside. He went to every farm his father had any interest in, cursing himself for not paying closer attention to his father's discussions of the extent of his estate. His distaste for country life had been so great that he had deliberately shut out any mention of his father's farming assets. Now he found that want of information a serious lack.

Nowhere that he went had anyone even heard of the Digbys, but by the end of the fortnight Andrew had formed a resolution. He would never set foot on the Wilmot property again. He would renounce his title, join the army as he had always planned, and nobility be damned! If he never saw his father's face again, so be it.

That night, his parents being away at a neighbor's for the weekend, he loaded up his horse with everything of value he could carry, including a sizable sack of heirloom jewels, and rode for London. He took with him a single servant, Megam, grandson of 'Lisbeth, a lad known for his wildness, who had often felt the brunt of Oliver Boyle's anger.

Arriving at the training center of London's "trained band," he sold enough assets to buy himself a commoner's commission and a soldier's position for Megam, and began his military career.

Meanwhile, in the Lincolnshire wheat country, the Digbys had settled in their new home. Lord Selden, unwilling to punish Philip for having sired a beautiful daughter, and castigating himself for having allowed Andrew such freedom with her for so many years, had secured a place for them on the estate of his wife's cousin, Simon Eliot, a member of the lower nobility who owed much to his more powerful in-law.

There Philip received the position of head mower, and his wife quickly adjusted to the larger cottage that her husband's greater prestige commanded. She soon forgot her tears in the excitement of marrying Lucy off to Peter Fletcher, a mower like her father. This simple young peasant was so in awe of Lucy's beauty and Philip's skill that he apparently did not notice that his firstborn son, christened Jeremy Digby Fletcher, arrived months earlier than he should have.

As for Lucy, no one asked how she felt, but her sisters and brothers, who knew her better than her busy mother ever had, noticed that her perennial cheerfulness had given way to a wistful melancholy that added a pallor beneath the rose of her cheeks and kept her from ever acquiring the rotund matronliness that her mother had attained early in her career as a mother. Always gentle, she often smiled but never laughed and was never known to be cross. Peter Fletcher was considered by all to be a fortunate man indeed, and no one believed it more than he.

Army life did not suit Andrew as he had thought it would. Despite his alleged hatred of the aristocracy, his years of being the pampered only son of an aristocrat had rendered him unfit for the kind of blind obedience demanded of an infantryman in His Majesty's army. Educated and clever, he had no patience with his superiors, whose slowness and pettiness rankled his impatient temperament. Their endless deliberations over matters that seemed obvious to him, and their refusal to heed his suggestions (What did he know, a mere enlisted man? Who did he think he was, putting on airs and trying to tell his betters what to do and affecting the accent and vocabulary of an aristocrat?) and the disdain of these commoners made him regret having been so hasty to break ties with his father, who would have bought him his own regiment to command.

Nevertheless, he knew he could never forgive his father for the loss of Lucy, and though he knew he could have done a better job than any of his superiors, he found that the army's work was really pretty boring. He soon saw that even the aristocrats who were commanding the troops had very little to do that was challenging except play politics, which he detested. Granted, there was no war going on in

England, but even in the event of war, which was always possible with the perennial religious conflicts on the Continent, he could tell after a few months in the army that the excitement of fighting would be dwarfed by the day-to-day boredom of the professional soldier. On that matter, at least, his father had been right: the army was not for him.

At first, he dealt with his disappointment by getting drunk every chance he got and by sabotaging his superiors' plans whenever he could, but he soon found that he was in no position to get away with behavior like that. One night he got drunk and tried to force himself on the barmaid of a tavern. Her father and brothers then beat him to a bloody pulp, and his superiors disciplined him for having created a public disturbance. After the unusually harsh sentence of two weeks on bread and water in the area of the camp's's dungeon that was reserved for delinquent soldiers, it was clear to him that stupid though he might consider his superiors, they still had authority over him and were in fact smart enough to take advantage of a situation in which they could take revenge on him for all the sabotage that they suspected but could not prove. Moreover, he was truly sorry for what he had tried to do to the girl after he had sobered up and realized that for all he knew, Lucy might have been in a similar situation and some drunken soldier might have been doing the same thing to her. As a result of all this, he decided that he would have to do something else to make the rest of his army hitch bearable.

His method was to try out each position that was available to an enlisted man. He tried working with the mess cooks, the artillery squad, the cavalry (where he excelled as a result of his background but left in frustration when he had to follow inane orders and was prohibited from trying the maneuvers that he knew only too well from his training on his father's estate), and the engineers (where his higher level of education and his haughty attitude antagonized both his superiors and his peers). Each group was happy to get rid of him when he applied for a transfer. He was too impatient, too sarcastic, too supercilious.

Finally it was supplies that saved him. After washing out of everything else, he was given a position on the quartermaster's staff and was able to observe first-hand the machinations of the merchants who supplied his regiment. Time after time he saw the merchants trick the supply sergeants into paying grossly inflated prices for their merchandise. They were able to do this because of the rampant ignorance of those doing the purchasing, who were often peasants from self-sufficient manors who had never had to deal with money. These men may have been shrewd enough back home when trading chickens for ducks, but they always got the worst end of the deal when bargaining with the very experienced merchants. Andrew quickly realized that all of the lessons he had so hated his tutor for had been truly practical after all. In this area as in all, he often tried to tell his superiors what they were doing wrong, but as usual, they would not listen. However, he was beginning to learn from observing the merchants that there were ways other than direct confrontation to get what one wanted from someone.

So his bided his time and gradually ingratiated himself with everyone on the quartermaster staff. Soon his superiors and co-workers forgot the abrasive, conceited young man he had been and began to trust him. In the meantime, he made friends with every merchant he could, even helping them, on occasion, to fleece the army, and receiving from them kickbacks that provided him with an income far above his regular soldier's pay. Thus, by the time his hitch was up at the end of four years, he had positions waiting for him with every merchant who supplied the army, as well as a nest egg with which to set himself up. Within a year, he himself was supplying the army, using his former friendships as his entrees and out-fleecing every merchant whom he had ever helped. By the time his thirtieth birthday rolled around, Andrew was a rich man.

Much of his wealth came from supplying the newly forming regiments of the Parliamentary army. Many of the commoners with whom Andrew had worked and ingratiated himself had become commanders in regiments forming to deal with the growing conflict between King Charles and Parliament. They all remembered him as he was in the later years of his hitch, when he was free with his money in the tavern, though he never drank much himself, and they all appreciated the "deals" he assured them he was giving their quartermasters in the name of their former friendship.

His other source of wealth, ironically, was the king's supporters. In dealing with these aristocrats, he was able to use to advantage the "knightly" training he had received as a youth. He knew how to speak their language, and in the turmoil of the times, they never stopped to ask themselves why. In providing them with what they needed, he often persuaded them to mortgage their lands, and eventually he was able to foreclose on those debts. This was a successful strategy, and by the time the conflict was all over, he had again become a landowner, without any help from his father.

Jeremy Fletcher was a problem for his parents almost from his birth. He adored his mother, but anything his father asked of him evoked a negative response. Like all farm boys, he was expected to do chores, feeding the livestock, milking the cow as soon as he was old enough, slopping the pigs. He hated them all.

Grooming the horses wasn't so bad, though. As a toddler, his mother had told him about a gallant knight on a fine white stallion who loved a princess who had been kidnapped and eaten by a fire-breathing dragon. He wanted to be that knight some day, and as he groomed the family's team, he could imagine himself galloping forth to his lady's castle.

It wasn't long, though, before the reality of being a poor mower's son sank in. Peter Fletcher wasn't as skilled as Phillip Digby, and his pay was much less. The family struggled with only one child, and often there was little to eat. Lucy became just a shadow of her former self. The hard work of a mower's wife and sorrow for her lost love left Lucy a wilted blossom, and she lost the two children she conceived after Jeremy. Finally, though, after a particularly good harvest, she managed to maintain a pregnancy, and Jeremy's sister, Emily, was born.

Another mouth to feed made life even harder for the family, and more and more chores fell upon Jeremy. Although Lucy had survived the pregnancy, she was far from the strong, rosy-cheeked girl she once was, and while Emily was little, Jeremy had to help his mother as well as doing his own work. Peter doted on Emily, who had the coloring and beauty that Lucy had once had. She, in turn, took advantage of her father's affection and blamed everything on Jeremy, who grew to resent both his sister and his father.

Peter tried to teach him to mow, and although he showed some of the skill that had made his grandfather so successful, his heart just wasn't in it. He loathed Peter. With the intellectual quickness he had inherited from Andrew, Jeremy found Peter's plodding deliberation exasperating, and when Peter fell for Emily's machinations time after time, Jeremy lost more and more respect for him until he couldn't stand to be in his presence.

Sometimes when he was sent into the town on errands, Jeremy saw soldiers in the streets. They looked so strong and confident with their swords and muskets and armor and their fine horses, and Jeremy admired them greatly. Each chance he got, he engaged them in conversation and gloried in their tales of the European wars. Before long, he decided that the army was where he wanted to be.

By the time Jeremy was sixteen, Emily was ten and was able to help her mother with the tasks that Jeremy had formerly undertaken. That meant more time in the fields for Jeremy and consequently more time with Peter. Familiarity did indeed breed contempt, and their relationship grew steadily worse. Jeremy rebelled against everything Peter asked him to do and often felt the cane across his back as a result. At this point, Jeremy's resentment was boiling within him.

One morning Jeremy did not come to the table for breakfast and was nowhere to be found. When he finally came home, he was badly hung over from a night of drinking in the town.

"Where have you been?" Peter demanded as Jeremy entered the house.

"With my friends," Jeremy answered, his eyes bleary and bloodshot.

"I'll friend you, you lazy, good-for-nothing lout!" shouted Peter, rising from the table and grabbing a walking cane that stood near the door. "I'll friend you, dancing in here as if you hadn't a care in the world while work waits outside. You won't be fit for anything for the rest of the day!"

Lucy ran to Peter, trying to pull him back to the table. "No, Peter, no!" she screamed. "Can't you see the boy's sick? He needs to be put to bed, not caned!"

Angrily, Peter slung Lucy from him, sending her crashing into the stairwell.

Emily ran to her mother, sobbing and screaming at her father. "No, Da, no! Don't! Don't!"

It was no use. When Peter got to Jeremy, he hit him so hard that the cane broke over Jeremy's back. Then he strode out and spent the rest of his anger on his work in the fields.

Jeremy's first thought was for his mother. He ran to Lucy and took her in his arms. "Ma, Ma, that man's a devil! We must get away from him before he kills us!" he pleaded. "I'm young and strong. I can take it, but now he's hurting you!"

Lucy pulled herself up to a sitting position. "I know, I know, Jeremy," she said, examining her son's back for the welts the cane had raised, "but where would we go? How would we live? We don't know any other life but this. How would we support ourselves?"

"I don't know, Ma, but we'd do something. Next time, he may kill one of us."

"Oh, he would never do that, Jeremy," Lucy insisted. "He really does love us. He's just worried about all that's going on in London. They say we may have a war."

"Ma, that's no excuse," Jeremy continued, "and you know it. I hate him. I want to take you away. Maybe we can go to the colonies.

You always said you wanted to."

"Jeremy, that's foolish talk," remonstrated Lucy. "It costs money to ride on a ship. We have nothing except what your da earns. Besides, I lost that chance before you were born. My fate is to be here."

Jeremy tried to argue, but he soon saw that he would never persuade his mother. However, that caning was the last straw for Jeremy. As soon as he recovered from his hangover, he ran away, hooking up with the first "trained band" regiment he came across.

At first, because of his youth, he could do little more than carry water to the horses and clean muskets for the soldiers, but unlike Andrew before him, he liked army life. It seemed so much more glamorous than farm life, and he found success in all he did. Even though he had ridden only plow horses, he rode well, and he soon found a place in a dragoon troop headed for combat against the Scots. Although it turned out to be a disastrous campaign for the English, as most of the forces were even greener than Jeremy, Jeremy distinguished himself and came to the attention of Captain Brian Johnson.

Back in Lincolnshire after the campaign, Jeremy returned home to find that his mother had died. He had truly loved his mother and grieved sincerely. He blamed Peter for her death. Emily told him that after he left, Peter had grown more and more violent, cursing Jeremy daily for leaving him with all the work. He stormed around the house, throwing things and never saying a civil word to anyone.

The stress of losing her son, whom she feared she would never see again, and Peter's constantly foul mood, began to tell on Lucy, and as the weeks passed, she began to wither and finally died, her heart broken.

For his part, Peter was inconsolable at losing her, it never occurring to him that he could have had any part in making it happen. In fact, he blamed her death on Jeremy. From being the envy of all the hands on the estate because of his beautiful, compliant wife, fine son, and lovely daughter, he became the object of everyone's pity.

Every time he saw Emily, he saw Lucy, and he spoiled her more and more.

Jeremy knew he could not exist in that environment, and he soon left.

By that time, however, he had all but exhausted his meager pay and was about to join a band of highwaymen who preyed on travelers (a common occupation for out-of-work soldiers), when Captain Johnson found him. The captain had engaged himself to recruit a regiment of horse to join the king's army in a campaign against the forces of Parliament. He asked Jeremy to join him, and Jeremy was only too glad to agree.

Part II

It was mid-afternoon at Waldby House, and the sky was clear for the first time that spring. Lady Diana Waldby sat in the arbor, awaiting the arrival of her old friend, Sophia Chapman. It had been years since the two had met, raising children and tending to their homes having taken precedence over visiting. Now their children were all grown, though, and they could take some time to relax. Sophia was to spend two weeks at Waldby House, and Diana was looking forward to reminiscing with her about their years together.

The two women, in their youth, had been ladies-in-waiting to the elderly Queen Elizabeth. Having arrived at court before even reaching puberty, Diana Woodcock and Sophia Penhurst had been awed, but mostly intimidated, by the splendor of the court of the virgin queen, by then well established as a monarch to be reckoned with. Their fathers and grandfathers, members of the minor gentry, had been supporters of Elizabeth's right to her father's throne and had lost their lands and almost their lives during the reign of Elizabeth's half-sister, Bloody Mary Tudor. After Mary's death, Elizabeth's gratitude prompted her both to return the lands seized by Mary and eventually to bring their daughters to her court, where she introduced them to the nobility of every country of Europe, and when the time came, saw that they were betrothed to good young men whom they loved and whose families the queen loved.

Unlike Elizabeth, who had sacrificed love for power, Diana and Sophia were happy to become just wives and mothers. Although they loved the queen like a mother and admired her inordinately, neither wanted to follow her chosen path, and the intrigue and danger of the court held no attraction for these country-bred girls. When Elizabeth died in 1603, the English court under James I changed drastically for the girls, now without their beloved elder monarch, and in 1606, when Henry Waldby and William Chapman led them away to their respective country estates, Diana and Sophia were glad to go.

For several years they saw each other when they went to London for the season, but soon the cares of home and family intervened, and they kept up with each other only by occasional letters.

The distance of years notwithstanding, Diana was sure that she and Sophia would pick up right where they had left off. As she sat on the arbor bench, from which she had a view of the drive down which Sophia's coach would come, Diana felt like a child again in her giddy anticipation of her friend's visit.

She wondered if William would accompany Sophia. Sophia's letter had not been very clear on that subject. To be sure, William should be, as Henry was, occupied with overseeing the spring plowing and lambing. In fact, it was because she had been so bored the year before while Henry was preoccupied with farming duties that Diana had decided to invite Sophia to come at that time, and she supposed that Sophia was also glad to have something to do. Sophia's letter had been so long in arriving that Diana did not have time to write back and ask. She had barely had time to prepare and, in her haste to do so, had really not stopped to think about it until now.

The letter said that Sophia's son, Richard, would be coming. But what might Richard like to do? Geoffrey was in Kent with the army, and Stephen was with his father at Split Oak cottage, thirty miles away, and wouldn't be back for a week at the soonest. Sally's husband, Alex, was nearby, but he too would be busy at this time of year. Only Judith was at home, Judith, who had been a bit of a tomboy as a youngster, preferring to play outside with Geoffrey and Stephen rather than staying indoors with Sally and playing with dolls. Now she was a young lady of seventeen, who thought only of laces and curls and Geoffrey's gallant army companions. At the least, she would have to prepare her daughter somewhat for the visit.

She found Judith in her chamber. Judith was sitting at her dressing table, and Clara, her maid, was carefully forming curls all over her head.

"My goodness, Judith," said Diana. "You will not have a hair left on your head if you keep making Clara fuss with it like that. Your hair was 'almost done,' you said—an hour ago!"

"Well, I didn't like it that way," said Judith, "so I made Clara do it over. It's your friend who's coming, Mamma, and I want to make a good impression."

"Judith, you're a beautiful young woman, and you'd be beautiful even if you dressed your hair like an Anabaptist," Diana said, admiring her daughter's raven-colored curls. "Ah, if I had had that skin and those eyes, every prince who visited Her Majesty's court would have fallen in love with me."

"Oh, Mamma," said Judith, "you're exaggerating."

"No, not a bit," said Diana. "Don't you know that Her Majesty's mother, Anne Boleyn, had looks like yours, only she was not nearly as pretty as you, and she swept King Henry right off his feet!"

"Oh, heavens, Mamma! Don't wish that on me!" cried Judith. "He had her beheaded!"

"Well, yes," said Diana, "but that was…. Well, never mind what that was. The point is, it has just occurred to me that Sophia may be bringing her son with her, and I want you to help to entertain him."

"Mamma!" cried Judith. "Isn't Lady Chapman's son a little boy? I have things to do. Geoff may be bringing one of his friends home with him after their training session. Clara and I have a lot of sewing to do if I'm to look presentable. I don't have time to play with a little boy!"

"Well, he's not exactly a little boy," said Diana, looking away so that her face would not be visible in Judith's mirror. "He's at least Stephen's age."

"Oh, heavens, Mamma! That's even worse!" cried Judith. "What on earth will I do with him? Boys that age want to hunt and run the dogs and things like that. I don't want to do those things!"

"Well, you used to like to do them," said Diana hopefully.

"Mamma, I was a little girl then," pleaded Judith.

"Look, Judith," said Diana. "I know this is an imposition, but Sophia is one of my oldest and dearest friends. If you can just put up with him until Stephen comes home. Please. You may find him to be very good company. Just ride with him a little, show him the place, and maybe play a little chess with him. Surely that's not too much to ask?"

"All right, Mamma, but just until Stephen gets back," said Judith. "And I won't be with him twenty-four hours a day. He'll have to entertain himself some of the time."

"All right, all right," said Diana. "Just be gracious about it. Try not to make him feel unwelcome."

"Mamma, I am a lady!" Judith cried. "I would never be impolite."

"I know, dear; I know," said Diana, smiling to herself as she thought of the temper tantrums that a younger Judith had thrown whenever she didn't get her way. "By the way, his name is Richard, if I remember correctly, after his grandfather. Sophia had only the one son, not two boys and two girls like me. I wonder if she wanted more?"

Her musings were interrupted by the pounding of hoof beats and the clanking of wheels on axles that signaled that the visitors had arrived.

Lady Chapman's carriage was visible from the window of Judith's chamber. The road was dusty, but Judith and Diana could catch glimpses of Lady Chapman's veiled head in the carriage window. A lone horseman rode alongside the carriage.

By the time Clara had finished Judith's hair to her satisfaction and Judith had reached the open front door of the house, Lady Chapman had descended from the carriage and was happily embracing her old friend. Her escort had also dismounted and was standing there, holding the reins of his horse and smiling at the two giggling women. He was blond and young, about Geoff's age, Judith guessed, with rosy cheeks showing above the still sparse facial hair.

Then the swishing of Judith's skirt caught his attention, and he looked up, meeting her inquiring gaze with the most beautiful blue eyes she had ever seen.

"Good afternoon," he said, bowing to her. "My name is Richard. Are you Sally or Judith? You look just like my mother said your mother looked when she was your age."

"I'm Judith," she said, feeling herself flush with embarrassment. "But...but...I thought you were Stephen's age! I was expecting a young boy!"

Now it was his turn to blush. "Oh. Well, I'm sorry to disappoint you, Judith," he said dejectedly. "I was hoping we'd get along."

"Oh, no, please," said Judith. "I didn't mean it that way. No, I'm glad you're not Stephen's age. I mean, I..."

Fortunately, Lady Chapman spied Judith at that point and diffused the awkwardness of the situation by coming over to embrace her.

"Oh, dear child," she cried, "you are the image of your mother. Diana, do you still have that green gown you wore the day King Philip came to court? If you put this child in it, she could be you! Now let's see, your name is...?"

"I'm Judith," said Judith, glad for the distraction. "It's so good of you to come, Lady Chapman. I feel as if I know you already; Mamma has spoken of you so often and so fondly."

"Oh, and I of her, dear child," said Lady Chapman. "What times we had together, Diana and I! Ah, the court of poor, drab King James, God save him, was nothing compared to Her Majesty's, and his son's is no better! What days those were! But I'm forgetting my manners. Diana, this is my son, Richard."

"Why, welcome, Richard," said Diana, embracing him. "What a handsome young man he is, Sophia. You must be so proud of him."

"Oh, Diana, he is the joy of my life!" said Lady Chapman, beaming. "And Judith, this is my son, Richard."

"Yes, Lady Chapman," said Judith, flushing again, "we have just met." She glanced quickly at Richard, and seeing that he was looking at her, lowered her eyes to avoid his.

"Well, well, come on in," said Diana. "You must be tired after your journey. You need a glass of sweet wine and a biscuit to revive your spirits. Come in! Come in! Judith, you run on ahead and tell Nancy to be stirring." She bustled them in, chattering all the while to Sophia. Richard, having handed the reins of his horse to the coachman, followed the ladies in. Judith, glad to escape, fled to the kitchen in search of Nancy.

"Why, Lady Judith," exclaimed Nancy when she saw Judith's flaming cheeks. "What in the world has happened?"

"Oh, Nancy, I'm so mortified," groaned Judith. "Lady Chapman has arrived with her son, and he's a man!"

"Aye," said Nancy, with a puzzled look on her face, "that's the case with most people's sons."

"But Nancy, Mamma said he was a boy! And I made such a fool of myself!"

"Oh, tut, Lady Judith," said Nancy, "surely a person may be mistaken without being thought a fool. Whatever you said, sure the gentleman took no offense."

"But Nancy, wait till you see him!" said Judith. "He's the handsomest young man I've ever seen, and all I could do was stand there and blush and say stupid things!"

"Ah, now we have it, eh?" smiled Nancy. "Our young lady has fallen in love!"

"Nancy!" cried Judith. "How dare you say such a thing?"

"Well, ma'am, that's how it usually happens," said Nancy, "just as you say. Been like that since Adam's day, I guess."

"But Nancy, I just met him!" cried Judith.

"Aye, and better acquaintance may change your mind," said Nancy, "but love it is at the moment, Lady Judith. 'Tis something I know when I see it. But they'll be wanting something to eat and drink. I'd best be stirring."

With that she disappeared into the pantry and left Judith to meditate on her words. By the time she got up the courage to join them in the parlor, she was more self-conscious than ever.

When she entered, Richard rose politely to greet her and handed her into a chair between himself and his mother. "I was hoping we'd continue to have the pleasure of your company," he said, relinquishing her hand slowly. "I was a bit concerned when you didn't come back."

"Oh, well, I had to make sure Nancy was really ready, you know," said Judith, hoping he wouldn't see the blush that she knew was forming again on her throat. "Only the best for my mother's dearest friend and her son." Nancy, who was pouring wine into Judith's mother's glass, turned and gave Judith a knowing wink, making her blush even more.

Further acquaintance did not change Judith's mind. As the two weeks progressed, she fell more and more in love with Richard, and his attentions to her made her feel that he felt the same. Instead of dreading going riding and doing things with him, she could not get enough of him. She rose at the crack of dawn, unusual for someone who normally slept later than the rest of the family, hoping to spend private time, and they talked or played chess far into the night. Through it all, Richard was a perfect gentleman, never presuming to take advantage of what Judith felt must be her obvious puppyish adoration of him.

Even when Judith's sister Sally and her husband Alex came to visit and brought news of conflict between the king and Parliament, Judith refused to be alarmed. What happened in London could stay in London.

Only at the close of the visit did Richard express, in a physical manner, the affection she hoped he was feeling. The night before his departure, he walked Judith up to her chamber after their chess game (their mothers having gone to bed long before) and, as she was opening the door and saying goodnight, instead of kissing her hand as he had done on other nights, he took her hand but then raised it to her own face, took her face in his hands, and kissed her gently on the lips. Then, himself blushing worse than she had done yet, he fled up the stairs to his own chamber.

The next morning, Judith was up before the sun, having hardly slept the night before. She did not want to miss even one minute of the time that remained of Richard's visit. She roused a very sleepy

Clara and made her light all the lamps in the room and get to work on her "toilette," as the French called it. It was a radiant and besplendored Judith who walked down to breakfast.

"My goodness, Judith," Lady Diana said when she saw Judith come in. "It's only eight o'clock in the morning, and you look as though you're going to the consecration of an archbishop!"

"Well, Mother," said Judith, tossing her head. "It's Lady Sophia's last morning here, and I wanted to look special for you old friend."

"And, I suspect, for her handsome son?" Lady Diana teased. "Don't think Sophia and I haven't noticed what's been going on between you two, Judith. However, we couldn't be more pleased!"

"Oh, Mother!" blushed Judith.

"Now, Judith, I've often told you that Sophia and I used to amuse ourselves imagining what it would be like if we each had a little girl and they became friends as we had been. When I realized that Sophia would have only the one boy, I thought our daydream would never come to pass. And now you and Richard! Why, it's just too delicious!"

"Mother!" pleaded Judith. "Don't jump to any conclusions. Richard and I have known each other for only two weeks. We hardly know anything about each…"

Her voice broke off at that point as the look on her mother's face caused her to whirl around to see Richard standing only a few feet behind her. The blush that had covered her face drained to stark paleness as she wondered how much of her mother's prattle Richard had heard.

"Of course, we know all about each other," said Richard, obviously trying to lighten yet another awkward moment. "We know we've had a wonderful time together these two weeks and that they're only the beginning of many more weeks ahead, that is, if you felt as I did."

"Oh, Richard, yes, of course I did," said Judith, her voice little more than a squeak. "I just meant…."

"That we shouldn't rush into things? That a friendship isn't built on just two weeks' acquaintance?" said Richard. "Why, I agree! We'll just have to see each other much more often if we're going to make our mothers happy. Would that suit you, Judith?"

"Well, yes, certainly," stammered Judith. Then, finally catching on to his facetiousness and matching the merriment in his eyes, she said, "Yes, that would suit me just fine. We will see each other as often as our mothers will let us and see if we can develop a friendship as strong as theirs." Reluctantly she turned her eyes from his and said to her mother, "Would that make you happy, Mother?"

"I heard that," said Lady Sophia, joining them in a swish of silk and lace. "And it certainly would make me happy! Diana, remember how we used to plan that our children would be friends just as we were? And here it is coming to pass. Oh, I'm so happy we came! Aren't you Richard? What a shame our visit has to be so short! But you must come to see us next time! Let's see, when will it be?"

A date two months hence was immediately set, and the four of them sat down to one of Nancy's finest breakfasts. Everyone was jolly and in the best of spirits at the prospect of their next meeting.

The mood was different, at least for Judith and Richard, when the time of the Chapmans' departure actually arrived an hour later. It was important that they get on the road early so as to reach Chapman Hall before nightfall on the third day. Colin brought Richard's horse around from the stable, with Lady Chapman's coachman driving her carriage right behind him.

As the Chapmans' belongings were loaded onto the carriage, the two old friends chattered happily away about their forthcoming visit, while Richard took Judith's hand and led her a bit apart where they could not be heard.

"Judith," he said, taking her other hand and facing her, "these were the most wonderful two weeks I've ever spent. I...." He looked at her solemnly, seeming to search her eyes.

"They were for me as well, Richard," Judith said, his humility making her bolder. "I've never met anyone like you," she said, letting her eyes meet his fully. "I didn't know being with a man could be so much fun!" Then, realizing how childish that must sound, she blushed and broke their eye contact.

Apparently he had not noticed anything childish about her remark. He brought her two hands up to his face and smothered them with kisses. His voice was cracking as he said, "Oh, Judith, dear, dear Judith!" and devoured her with his eyes.

"Richard! Time to go!" Lady Chapman's voice sounded far away to Judith. She was lost in Richard's eyes, lost in the touch of his lips on her hands.

Then the moment was gone, and Richard was on his horse, waving as he rode away. She waved to him with her handkerchief until he was completely out of sight. Lady Diana stood beside her, herself furiously waving goodbye to her old friend, the tears streaming down her face.

"Oh, Judith," she said, "you don't know how much these two weeks have meant to me. It's as if God has given me back my girlhood in the person of Sophia! Oh, I just can't wait for our visit to Chapman Hall. I think I'll have to go to my closet and cry awhile. Excuse me, please, will you, dear?"

"Of course, Mother," Judith said, delighted to have time to be alone with her thoughts. The two of them walked back into the house arm in arm, and Judith went up to her room, spending the rest of the day lolling on her bed and daydreaming until her lack of sleep the night before got the better of her and she dozed off into a sound sleep full of dreams of Richard.

"Mistress Judith! Mistress Judith!" The sound of Clara's voice brought her back to the reality that Richard was gone and she would not see him for two months. She almost wept.

"What is it, Clara? What's the matter?" she asked groggily.

"Why, nothing's the matter, Mistress," said Clara. "Your mother wants you to come down to the parlor, that's all."

"Oh, all right," said Judith. "Will you help to put me back to rights? Though I guess it doesn't matter, now that they're gone."

"Oh, Mistress, I don't blame you," cooed Clara. "Such a

handsome young gentleman. You'll make such a pretty pair going down the aisle. I'll bet even the vicar, that old sour face, will smile!"

"Down the aisle!" cried Judith. "What are you talking about, Clara?"

"Why, you know, Mistress, you and Sir Richard (that's to be), when you get married."

"Married? Who said anything about getting married?" exclaimed Judith, bouncing up to a sitting position in the bed.

"Why, your mother did, Mistress," said Clara. "That's what Nancy said. She said that.... Excuse me, Mistress, but I must be off." In a wink, Clara was out of the room.

"Clara, come back here this instant!" cried Judith. "Clara!"

Clara looked up from a hanging head as she slunk back into the doorway. "Yes, Mistress?" she said, her voice almost a whisper.

"Clara, how dare you leave the room without my permission!" cried Judith. "What could have been so important that you had to leave in mid-sentence?"

"Well, Mistress, it's just that I...." Clara's form disappeared again around the door jamb.

"Clara, come here right now!" said Judith. "And don't you leave again until I have finished with you. Do you want me to have Papa send you back to your father's cottage to work in the dairy again?"

"Oh, no, Mistress, not that!" shuddered Clara. "You know the very sight of a cow makes me tremble, so much do I hate them."

"Well, then, finish what you were telling me," said Judith, getting up from the bed and sitting at her dressing table. "You can talk and do my hair at the same time. You're always babbling away at your combing and pinning."

"But Mistress, if I tell you, then I'll likely end up in the dairy anyway. Once Nancy finds out I told! Oh, and once your mother finds out Nancy told me! Oh, Mistress, please don't make me tell!" pleaded Clara into the mirror.

"Clara, this is nonsense. If something's afoot regarding a marriage for me, I deserve to know about it, don't you think?" said

Judith coaxingly, all the while fully believing that Clara and Nancy had just been off on one of their romantic fantasies.

"Well, Mistress, I thought you knew by now, or I would never have opened my mouth," said Clara. "Oh, Mistress, if I tell, promise you won't let them send me back to the dairy! Please! Please!"

"All right, all right!" said Judith. "Why, this news is taking longer to come than a birthday to a child! Out with it!"

"Well, you see, Mistress, it was this way—says Nancy, mind you, not I. It seems that the letter your mother got from Lady Chapman contained a proposal of marriage between you and Sir Richard (to be)."

"What?" shrieked Judith.

"Now, Mistress," said Clara calmingly, "now that I'm wound up, let me spin my top. As I was saying, Lady Chapman wrote to ask for your hand in marriage for her son, provided, of course, that the two of you liked each other."

"Clara, do you mean to say that this whole visit was planned just so Richard and I could 'examine the wares,' as a peddler might say?" said Judith, incredulous.

"Oh, yes, Mistress, and well planned too. Your mother arranged for it to take place at a time when none of your brothers were home, and your father neither, so that Sir Richard (to be) would have to spend all his time with you."

"But Clara, this is terrible! Was Richard in on all of this?" Judith's heart was sinking lower and lower in her chest.

"Oh, no, Mistress!" said Clara. "This little stew was cooked up by your two mothers. Needless to say, your mother was pleased as pie when she found out that her old friend wanted her son to marry you. From what Nancy says, they've been sending letters back and forth for months. Nancy says your mother is already planning what she'll wear to the wedding. She's planning a trip to London to buy the silk, and…."

"Oh, this is horrible!" said Judith. "My own mother plotting against me!"

"No, Mistress," said Clara, "not at all! Why, Nancy says that in some families like yours, the young ladies and gentlemen are just told by their parents whom to marry! Sometimes even the king makes their choice for them when they're just babies!"

"Well, and what if Richard and I hadn't liked each other?" demanded Judith.

"Well, what Nancy said was that's why your mothers didn't tell. They didn't want to have bad feelings between their children if nothing worked out. Besides, according to Nancy, you mother wasn't really sure how old Sir Richard (to be) really was. She thought he was younger than you and it would take a while before he was old enough to fall in love and you were grown up enough for your mother to part with you."

Judith had heard enough. She flew from the room, ignoring Clara's protests that her hair was not yet finished, and stormed into the parlor.

"Mother!" she shrieked. "What has been going on?"

"I beg your pardon!" said Diana, turning from her seat at her writing table. "What is all this noise about?"

"Mother, Clara just told me about your little plot to make a match between Richard and me!" Judith yelled. "How dare you!"

"Judith, I will not have you speak to me that way!" said Diana as calmly as she could make herself. She knew that Judith's high spirit was one of her most attractive qualities, but sometimes it could be irritating. She said no more, just looking at Judith expectantly, her lips pursed, not quite in a frown. Her composure was effective, as usual, with Judith. ("Water puts out fire," her husband often said when she handled Judith that way).

"I'm sorry, Mother, but I'm just so angry!" Judith said, her voice less shrill but still not back to its usual timbre.

"Well, what's there to be angry about?" demanded Diana. "Would you have preferred to know what Sophia and I were hoping? Would it have been better to be put on the spot? What if you hadn't liked him?"

"But Mother, there I was being my usual idiotic self, and Richard was looking me over, like Father does when he goes to the stock auction!"

"Judith, what a thing to say!" cried Diana. "Surely you can't think that Richard saw you only as livestock!"

"Well, he knew what he was here for, which is more than I did!" shrieked Judith.

"Oh, no, dear, he didn't," said Diana. "He didn't know any more than you did. We didn't want either of you to feel bad or to feel pressured. We just wanted you to meet and see what happened."

"You mean Richard acted the way he did without knowing his mother wanted him to marry me?" said Judith, her eyes huge.

"Yes, that's exactly what I mean," said Diana. "He thought he was being given time off from helping his father so that his mother wouldn't have to travel alone. Sophia and I promised each other that we wouldn't mention the word marriage to either one of you. We'd wait until you brought it up yourselves, if that ever happened. And that's just what would have been the case if someone I know hadn't opened her big mouth. There are really big ears around here, too! I haven't spoken to anyone about this except your father. I wonder who was eavesdropping!"

"Well, you can ask Clara if you want to," said Judith. "After she let the cat out of the bag, she wouldn't tell me the rest until I promised she wouldn't be sent back to the dairy."

"I'll see to her later," said Diana, "but come now, don't you think our plan was a good one? You and Richard enjoyed each other's company without a bit of pressure, and everything happened just the way Sophia and I hoped it would."

"I can't see how you can say that," said Judith. "I would never have brought up the topic of marriage with Richard."

"What?" cried Diana, springing to her feet and facing her daughter. "After all the time you spent with Richard, you don't want to marry him?"

"Well, you told me I'd have to entertain him until Stephen came home, and I did it, didn't I?" said Judith, smirking.

"Oh, Judith, surely you don't mean to tell me that all those blushes, all those wide eyes and giggles were just your way of doing your duty?" Diana could tell by Judith's face that she was lying. Judith had never been able to dissemble. Her heart was always an open book. "It's all right to admit that you liked him, Judith. He liked you too. He told his mother that the last two weeks here had been the best of his life."

"He did?" cried Judith, her cheeks and neck on fire.

"He did, indeed," said Diana, smiling knowingly. "I wouldn't be at all surprised if he brought up the subject of marriage as soon as they got home and he could speak to both of his parents together."

"But Mother, I'm only seventeen years old!" cried Judith. "I really do like Richard, but I haven't had anyone to compare him to. What if there are other men that I'd like better?"

"Oh, you are sensible and practical, aren't you?" said Diana. "Doesn't emotion count with you at all? I've never seen anything like it. When I was your age, I thought each man I fell in love with was the answer to all my prayers. I never gave a second thought to the fact that he might not be the right one for me or that there might be someone else I'd like better later."

"Well," said Judith, "it seems to me that what you said just proves that I'm right."

"What do you mean?" said Diana.

"I mean that you said you fell in love with several men. I have fallen in love with only one! Don't I get a chance to try out a few others?"

Diana was a bit taken aback by the dispassionate way her daughter discussed relationships, but she certainly could see Judith's point. What if they married Judith off too soon, and she grew to hate Richard or, worse still, to fall in love with someone else after she was married? Diana had seen that happen often enough while she was at court, and she had seen heads roll because of it.

"You're right," she said to Judith. "You should have a chance to meet other young men and to make sure you find the right one. I will not urge you to rush into anything, and if Sophia questions that, I'll say that your father has insisted. I'm sure he will anyway."

"Thanks, Mamma," said Judith, giving her mother a hug and heading for the door. "I guess I forgive you for deceiving me. And I did enjoy being with Richard."

The truth was, Judith could not think of anything else except Richard, but she was determined not to let her mother know. Two could play at this deception game. If there was anything she could not stand, it was to be manipulated. Even though in this case the manipulation had worked, she had resolved to have the last word, and she felt she had gotten it.

The two months that elapsed between the Chapmans' visit to Waldby House and the Waldbys' visit to Chapman Hall could have been the longest in Judith's life, so eager was she to see Richard again. Instead, they passed very quickly, completely taken up with preparations for the trip. There were dresses to make, hairstyles to try out, names of the members of the Chapman household and their neighbors to memorize. Clara complained constantly that her fingers hurt, but Judith didn't care. Judith found little time to be alone with her thoughts, but when she was, they were all of Richard.

Finally the day of departure came. Judith, Diana, Clara, and Audrey (her mother's personal maid) climbed into the coach and were off, accompanied by Stephen, who was none too happy about missing the summer activities that always followed the planting season but looked forward to meeting Richard, about whom he had heard much from his family and the servants.

Whereas the time of preparation had flown, the trip itself seemed interminable to Judith. The beauty of the English countryside in June left her unmoved as she squirmed and fanned herself in the stifling heat of the coach with its tiny windows.

It took three days to reach Chapman Hall. Geoffrey had told her that they could have covered the distance in two or horseback, but it would have been undignified for ladies in a coach to try to go that fast. That meant two nights in the homes of friends and relatives.

At Moncton Manor, the home of her mother's cousin, Margaret Bolling, she enjoyed meeting Margaret's son, Edward, but charming though he was, he did not hold a candle to Richard in her eyes. His brother, Michael, whom Geoffrey had always liked, had become too much the farmer for Judith. She couldn't imagine his being comfortable anywhere but in the fields or sheepcote.

The second night found them at the home of one of the Chapmans' cousins, John Chapman, who had only daughters. Two were teenagers, one, Mary, exactly Judith's age, and they got along well, but they were so complimentary of everything about Judith that she was fairly sure they were insincere. Being rather moody herself, Judith could not believe that people could be that cheerful and positive all the time.

Finally, on the third day, they came out of a curve through a copse of trees and saw Chapman Hall in the distance. The sight took Judith's breath away. The rolling Yorkshire countryside lay before them, and on a hill sat the stone house, sprawling out between its towers that must have been hundreds of years old. The stone was dark and somewhat forbidding, but as they approached, Judith could see that the Chapmans must be very wealthy indeed, as the walls of each floor of the house were graced by glass-filled windows, the small panes of glass held together with strips of lead. An avenue of trees led up to a terrace that ran almost the full length of the south side of the house.

"Oh, look, Judith," cooed Diana. "Sophia has latticed windows! I'm so jealous."

"I'm sure the house must be bright inside," commented Judith, "but I'll bet it's also cold in the winter."

"Well, perhaps the windows are only on the south side. It would be very nice to have the southern warmth to cheer you. Nevertheless, I think our house looks more gracious, don't you?"

A muttered "Mumpf" was Judith's only reply.

After that, they rode in silence, taking in the specifics of their surroundings. The road led around the east side of the house and down the hill a bit, then up again on the north side to a circular drive through the immaculately kept formal garden, which was awash with spring flowers. Large trees shaded parts of the spacious lawn, and a stone outbuilding with an opening large enough for a carriage announced its purpose. All four women in the coach were on the edges of their seats, peering out of the windows.

"Might this be my home some day?" Judith mused to herself. The thought sent a shiver of excitement through her.

Midway up the drive, a rider on horseback emerged to greet Stephen, who had ridden ahead: Richard. Judith felt a knot rise in her throat. Would she feel the same as at Waldby House, or had she only been dreaming that Richard was wonderful.

"Lady Diana, Judith, how glad we are that you've come," Richard called through the window of the coach, barely glancing at Diana but holding Judith's eyes with his own as long as the moving coach and his horse would allow.

Then they stopped in front of the double doors that were the house's main entrance. While Stephen let his mother out of one side of the coach, Richard opened Judith's door and extended his hand. With utter abandon of all the rules of polite behavior, Judith flew into his arms. If he was surprised, he didn't show it. He engulfed her warmly and likely would have kissed her as well, but the brim of her traveling hat got in the way.

Their embrace was interrupted by the arrival of Lady Sophia on the doorstep. "Diana, finally you've made it to my home. I've been on pins and needles all day. John sent a rider, so we knew you'd probably reach us today. Oh, Judith, what a lovely traveling costume. Isn't youth wonderful, Diana? She looks as fresh as a daisy!" Judith beamed in the glow of Sophia's compliments, and so did Clara, who had worked long hours on that traveling costume.

After hugs from Sophia, the guests were ushered into the house and whisked up to their rooms by the servants to wash up and change out of the traveling clothes. Diana and Judith were given a room up a single flight of stairs with only one door near the stair landing, clearly a guest room. The walls were covered with framed panels of dark wood, and the canopied bed was intricately carved with vines and grapes and hung with heavy silk curtains. A fireplace stood ready, decorated with panels showing portraits of dramatic characters. There was a commode chair as well. The room had a bay window with two tiers of windows that let in the sunlight to reveal the ceiling elaborately carved in fruited vines, flowers, and animal heads in pastel colors. Judith had never seen so elegant a room. Waldby House had wood-paneled walls, too, as they were what replaced tapestries for warming up old stone houses, but this room went far beyond anything at home.

Meanwhile, Sophia and Richard saw to laying out a feast of oat bread, aromatic and creamy local cheeses made of the milk of their own sheep, the finest wines, and the summer's first fruits. These were served not in the dining room but in a lovely parlor near the front doors, again with a large window that brightened the dark paneling.

Judith would have liked just to nibble and preserve some semblance of ladylike behavior, but she was too hungry and thirsty. As she ate, Richard, who was seated between Judith and her mother, found a million excuses to lean over to ask Judith some mundane question. The look in his eyes as they met hers was as hungry as she felt regarding the food. "Could I ever be as necessary to him as food is to me," thought Judith, "or will I be just a passing fancy? Will I get to the point where he's more necessary to me than food?"

The two weeks at Chapman Hall passed much too quickly for Judith. Sophia had so much to share with them, so many parties, so many ladies' activities, that Judith and Richard were able to spend very little time together. Moreover, Richard was occupied with entertaining Stephen, who came to respect and admire Richard in ways he had never done with Geoff. By the time they left, Stephen, without any prompting from anyone, was encouraging Judith to marry Richard just so that he could spend time with the older young man.

In both the public and the few private moments Judith and Richard had, she came more and more to appreciate him. At the height of the visit, Sophia hosted a soiree to which all the neighboring gentry were invited. It was held in the dining room that made up the entire center of the house, soaring up three stories and stretching from the front wall to the back terrace. The south wall of this room was mostly a window that went from table height up to where a second story would have been ceiled had there been one. The candles that flickered on the wide windowsill illuminated the stained glass shields of families associated with the house throughout its many years each adorning its own window section. The beauties of the room were duly noted by Diana, who complimented Sophia on her design of the room, which was recently renovated by Sophia.

Judith barely noticed her surroundings. Her eyes were on only Richard. He danced beautifully and with gusto; he was reserved without being stuffy, playful without being boisterous. Even when the room was full of young men, everyone's eyes, not just hers, went straight to him. It was quite obvious from their reactions that all the nearby young ladies wanted him and were not pleased that he paid so much attention to Judith.

As the visit progressed, she was craving more of him and not getting it. One night as Clara was brushing her hair after an especially busy day of socializing, Judith said, "Well, if my mother and Lady Sophia really want Richard and me to marry, they certainly are making it difficult for us, keeping us otherwise occupied all the time."

"Just like that story Colin told me about from Master Stephen's book, the one where the hungry man would reach out for some food and it would disappear," replied Clara.

"Oh, no, Clara," Judith began, turning around to face Clara. "That was Tantalus in Greek mythology. That has nothing to do with us."

"No?" said Clara. "Well, it seems the same to me."

What if it was? wondered Judith. What if this was part of the "plan" as well? She could just hear her mother saying, "All right, Judith, we'll see how much you want to 'shop around' for a husband."

That realization made Judith even more adamant about meeting other men before deciding on Richard, despite the fact that the more she was with him, the more she liked him. She wouldn't have her future decided for her that easily.

Finally, on the last day of the visit, the activities came to a halt, and she was able to be alone with Richard. They went out riding so that he could show her the beauties of the estate, and she found the forests, fields, meadows, rolling hills, and valleys of the West Yorkshire countryside to be beautiful indeed.

"All of this will be mine, someday," Richard was saying. "I only hope I can prove worthy of it. My father has put his heart and soul into this land, as my mother has into Chapman Hall."

"Oh," said Judith, "I'm sure you'll rise to the occasion. Your father has many years left to live, a long time for you to learn what you need to learn."

"That's true," said Richard, "but he's getting tired. He and I had a long conversation not long before you arrived, and he told me that when I marry and have my first child, he plans on turning over this estate to me. He and my mother will move to one of my mother's properties farther south, and he will devote his time to breeding better varieties of sheep."

"Are you serious? Won't your mother be devastated to leave this beautiful home on which she's worked so hard?"

"I'm sure she will miss it," said Richard, "but my father says she is actually looking forward to having a new home to decorate. She wants to oversee the building of it herself and do exactly what she wants, not having to cope with an ancient house, trying to put her own stamp on other people's designs. She tried adding onto the house to make it more symmetrical, but she just hasn't been able to make herself do anything with it. We still live mostly in the section next to the old tower."

"Well, that makes sense," said Judith. "I think the women of our parents' generation care greatly about their surroundings. Personally, I've never thought much about it. I guess I'm too much of a tomboy to be concerned about decorating a house. To me, a house is just a place to share with those you love."

"So, could you live in an old rambling place like this if you had loved ones living in it?" asked Richard, lifting an eyebrow.

"Of course, I could," replied Judith. "If I loved someone, I could live in a hovel with him."

"Well, I'm guessing there's not much chance of that," chuckled Richard. "I know that your parents are sufficiently comfortable that you and your siblings will never lack anything."

"True," said Judith. "That was just a figure of speech. The point I was making is that it's the people who make the home, not the house."

"I couldn't agree more," said Richard, reining his horse. "Let's rest awhile under that tree and let the horses have a nibble."

He helped her down from her mount, grabbed a cloth from his saddlebag, and led her into the shade of an old oak with limbs almost touching the ground. They sat on the cloth in silence for a few moments, not looking at each other.

When the silence became as heavy as lead, they turned to each other. "Judith," Richard said.

Then she was in his arms, on her back, each of his kisses exploding like stars in her head, their breaths faster and faster. She felt his hand travel down her hip and leg to the hem of her dress but made no protest.

Suddenly Richard let go of her and sat up. Still panting, she blurted, "Richard, what's wrong? Did I do something wrong?"

Richard turned around and looked into her panicked face, his eyes soft. "No, my darling, you did everything right. That's why we have to stop. You are too precious to me to be treated this way. Come, let's go back."

They rode in silence back to Chapman Hall. Judith's feelings were a muddle of desire, hurt, and puzzlement. Her brain just couldn't sort it all out.

When they reached the house, Richard saw her to the door and disappeared. He did not appear for dinner, and she did not see him the rest of the evening. She cried herself to sleep that night, unable to understand what had happened between them.

The next morning, at their departure time, he arrived. He had dark circles under his eyes just like Judith's, and she wondered if he also had cried himself to sleep. Smiling, he bade Diana and Stephen a warm goodbye and wished them a safe and pleasant trip, while Judith just stood to the side, embarrassed and feeling ignored. Finally, he came over to her and took her gloved hands in his, lifted them to his face and kissed them. "Be safe, my precious Judith," he said, his eyes devouring hers, "until we meet again."

"Th-thank you, Richard," Judith stammered. "We've had a wonderful visit." She could say no more. She bolted into the coach without waiting for a hand-up and turned her face away so that he couldn't see the blush and the tears.

She was very grateful that her mother chattered away with Audrey and Clara instead of trying to engage her in conversation, leaving her alone with her thoughts.

She could not for the life of her figure out Richard's behavior. One minute he was treating her as if she were the most important thing in the world to him; the next, he was rejecting her, not talking, and disappearing. Was he "strange," in some way? Was he just being nice to her sometimes to please his mother? Did he just want to "have his way" with her? Did he stop out there under the tree because her father might kill him if he found out? Judith's seventeen-year-old head could not pierce the fog of these questions, and the ride home was not at all pleasant. The joviality of their hosts along the way was galling to someone who felt as she did, and her mother had to remind her to be polite.

Once home, Judith threw herself into the routine of the house. For the first time, she began to notice how the house was run. She actually listened as her mother gave instructions to Nancy in the kitchen, and she watched what Nancy was doing, asking questions of both her mother and Nancy that surprised them both. She followed Colin around the grounds, observing his tasks and asking more questions. She badgered Clara with questions about her home life, questions Clara was loath to answer, believing it not to be her place to share such information with the young lady of the house. When her father retired to his closet after dinner and began going over his farm records, she looked over his shoulder, wondering what each item in his ledger meant.

When her sister Sally and Alex, her husband, came over to visit, she cornered Sally and demanded to know what married life was like. Sally was amused at her little sister's questions but shared only superficial information with Judith, not the meaty information Judith really wanted but didn't know how to articulate.

This went on for a week and a half.

Then one morning after breakfast, Judith heard hoof beats on the driveway. Curious, she looked out of the window and immediately recognized Richard. Terrified that he might be the bearer of bad news about someone in his family, she rushed out to meet him before her mother noticed him so that she could break the bad news to her mother if something had happened to Sophia. All of her awkwardness regarding Richard was abandoned in her concern for the welfare of his family and her mother.

Richard was flushed from his ride and dismounted only long enough to kiss Judith's hand perfunctorily and ask the whereabouts of her father. Judith wasn't sure in which field her father was working, so she had to find her mother and ask. Of course, Diana wanted Richard to come in for refreshments and a visit, but Richard insisted that his errand was pressing and rode off in the direction Diana had specified.

"Well, I wonder what that's all about!" said Diana with her hands on her hips as the dust of Richard's horse's hoofs settled. "Whatever it was, surely it could have waited until he had a bit to eat and drink, I would think."

"He did seem to be in a terrible hurry," said Judith. "I hope nothing bad has happened at Chapman Hall."

"Oh, I wouldn't think so," said Diana. "If it had, Richard would have to stay there and deal with it. He would have sent one of the servants."

Judith hadn't thought of that. She felt so childish and embarrassed, just running out to meet him like that. What must he think of her? Just when she was beginning to get over what had happened during her visit to Chapman Hall, this happened and put her back into a state of melancholy.

When Judith's father returned to the house two hours later, he was alone. From the doorway, Diana looked at him with her eyebrows knit.

"Where's Richard?" she inquired, with her hands on her hips. "You didn't put him to work out there, did you?"

"No, of course not, Diana," replied Sir Henry. "I sent him over to Sally and Alex's for the night. We have to talk, you and I." His face was serious but calm, so Diana followed him silently into their bedroom.

Judith had witnessed all of this and was mightily confounded. A thousand questions raced through her head, all of them portending the worst. She paced like a pent-up horse for the half hour her parents' door was closed. Eavesdropping occurred to her, but she respected her parents' privacy too much to stoop to that.

Finally the door opened, and her parents emerged. Their faces told her nothing. She looked for signs of good news and bad news and found neither. It was a though both parents were wearing stiff wooden masks.

"Judith," her father finally said. "We need to talk to you. Please come into the study."

The study! That was the room where justice was administered. When Judith was a child, gross misbehavior, like the time she broke an expensive round window glass with Stephen's slingshot, was punished. Although she was only seven at the time, she never forgot the humiliation of being spanked by her father with the back of a wooden hairbrush. Her mother had pulled up her skirt and had stood by while her father hit her ten times. The physical hurt was negligible, but the embarrassment was lasting.

What had she done this time? Surely Richard would not have ridden all the way here to report that he felt slighted because she barely told him goodbye! Could it have been what happened under the tree? Did he hate her now because she had so eagerly succumbed to his kisses? Did he think her a trollop?

"Judith," her father began, "you know of your mother's hopes that you would marry the son of her good friend. I concurred in those hopes once I met Richard. However, we both understood your reluctance to rush into anything. Marriage is meant to be forever, and it should not be entered lightly.

"It had been our intention to take you to London, where you could meet many young men, enjoy yourself, and then, later, make a choice about whom you would marry, subject to our approval, of course.

Judith opened her mouth to reply, but her father continued.

"Unfortunately, the strife between King Charles and Parliament has cast a pall over our plans. The next few years are likely to be difficult ones for England. None of us knows what the future will bring."

Judith was in agony, imagining the worst. What did her father mean? Had Richard brought some dire news about the king? Would the fanatics come and kill them all? She felt so selfish worrying about what Richard thought of her when the matter at hand was obviously of so much greater import.

"Fortunately, however," her father continued, "you will have the chance, if you so choose, to have some happiness in the meantime. Richard has asked for your hand in marriage."

Judith felt the blood leave her face. Richard still wanted her? He wanted her with him even through this trouble? Did that mean he really loved her? Could she be a good wife to him? Could she make better for him the pain that might come?

"Judith!" her mother chided. "Your father just spoke to you. Did you not understand what he said?"

Regaining her composure a little, Judith whispered, "Yes, I understood him. At least, I think I did."

"Well?" demanded Sir Henry. "Will you have him or not? I told him that the decision was yours."

Judith looked into her father's eyes and then her mother's, her own eyes filling with tears. How good her parents were! How they cared about her! They were letting her choose her own husband, something that almost never happened to girls in her position.

And they were offering her the most wonderful man she had ever met, a man who made her heart flutter and her pulse race every time she saw him, a man to whom she would gladly have lost her virginity if his decency had not intervened.

"Well?" said her mother.

Leaving behind the thoughts, both delightful and ashamed, of her last encounter with Richard, Judith finally spoke. She knew her cheeks were burning as she said, "Yes, I will have him. I cannot imagine spending my life with anyone but Richard." She rose and hugged and kissed her parents. "Not only do I have the best parents who ever lived; now I will have the best husband who ever lived!"

"Odds bodkins, Diana, I do believe we've raised a child with sense!" her father chuckled. "Well, I'd best fetch Richard. He'll want to receive this news and join his bride to be."

"Oh, Judith, you've made me so happy!" cooed Diana. "I know you and Richard will make the most wonderful couple." With that, Diana launched into a hurricane barrage of wedding plans, dresses, parties, and guest lists, none of which Judith even heard. Her thoughts were all on Richard.

An hour later, her father and Richard appeared in the courtyard. Judith had been rehearsing in her mind what she would say to him when she saw him. Each scenario she proposed to herself seemed inadequate to the occasion, and she rejected one after the other.

As it turned out, all her planning was unnecessary. As soon as the door to the study, where her mother had told her to wait, opened and she saw Richard, she threw all caution to the winds and rushed into his arms. He held her tightly, then went down on one knee. "Judith, your parents have given me permission to ask you—will you be my wife?"

"Yes, yes, I will, Richard, with all my heart!" Judith exclaimed, lifting him up and pulling him to her.

Richard kissed her tenderly and then pushed her away slightly. "I have something for you," he said. He pulled from his vest pocket a velvet pouch and from it removed the most beautiful ring Judith had ever seen. Brilliant green emeralds surrounded a huge sapphire, and the gold of the setting shone like the sun. "My father gave this to my mother when he asked her to marry him, and now my mother wants you to have it."

"Oh, Richard, it's so beautiful. I don't know what to say," stammered Judith.

"In saying you'll marry me, you've already said everything," laughed Richard. "You've granted my most earnest prayer."

"And your asking made my dearest wish come true," said Judith. "After our ride and what happened, I thought you'd never want to see me again," she said, searching his eyes.

"Oh, Judith, stopping and leaving that day was the hardest thing I ever did. You were so beautiful, so giving, and so innocent.

I knew I had to marry you quickly before I gave in and ruined you. If something scandalous had come between us, I would never have forgiven myself."

"Dear, dear Richard," was all Judith could say. She had been cursing her impetuous nature, but somehow God had made it all come out all right.

Then began the preparations for the wedding. Because Richard and Judith and their families were all members of the gentry, contracts had to be drawn up settling the questions of dowry and other financial arrangements. Those for this wedding were completed more quickly than many since the families were friends and of similar financial and property standing. Nevertheless, the solicitors kept the roads hot between Waldby House and Chapman Hall until finally the papers signed by the parents and prospective spouses were officially filed and the king had granted permission for the marriage to go forward.

Next came the betrothal ceremony, or "spousals." Judith and Richard committed themselves to each other orally before an audience of both families and all the noble neighbors nearest Waldby House. To show her appreciation for Lady Sophia's ring, which she would wear on the ring finger of her left hand until the wedding, Judith wore a two-piece dress of sapphire silk trimmed with emerald lace. It was her first time to wear a farthingale, which she found uncomfortable but which Diana insisted fashion demanded. She had to lean over it even to touch Richard.

At the time of the promises, Richard placed on the ring finger of Judith's right hand the lower half of the "gimmel" ring. Then Judith placed the upper half on his pinkie finger. The ring was in three parts. The upper and lower parts, made of gold, would fit together over the middle part, also of gold, but with a ruby heart attached. On their wedding day, the vicar, who would keep the third part until that time, would put the three parts together, and Richard would put them on Judith's finger. At that point, the open golden hands that protruded from the upper and lower parts would fit together over the heart, which would no longer be visible.

Judith was acutely aware that, having gone through spousals, she and Richard were legally free to consummate their union, but Richard did not suggest it, and Judith was glad. She had many questions to ask before taking such a big step, and she did not want weeks of separation from Richard to follow that big step, weeks during which both households would prepare for the wedding itself. She also did not want to be pregnant at the wedding. Sally had been, and she had been nauseated throughout the wedding.

Although Judith did some of the sewing of her wedding gown and her trousseau herself, it was mostly Clara and seamstresses brought in from the surrounding towns who created the dress that she eventually wore. Sally, with her auburn hair and green eyes, had worn a gown of russet silk, russet being one of the customary colors for brides. With her dark hair and fair skin, Judith chose white instead. After her discomfort at the spousals, she was determined not to wear a farthingale, and she finally convinced Diana that such devices were out of style when one of Diana's London cousins sent a drawing of one of Queen Henrietta Maria's latest frocks, which had no farthingale. This drawing became the inspiration for Judith's dress.

The bodice of the dress was white brocade, with threads of the palest blue woven throughout. The brocade extended into a sharp point in front, merging with a panel of the same fabric that spread in a triangle shape down the front of the skirt. The skirt was full, made of heavy white peau de soie, and Judith agreed to wear voluminous petticoats beneath it to show its fullness to advantage as long as the gathers on the petticoats started at least six inches below her waist.

The bodice came to a point in the back as well, and from it flowed a train of the same fabric as the bodice.

The sleeves, which were made of the same white peau de soie as the skirt, were tied to the bodice at the shoulders with pale blue ribbons. Superimposed upon the upper portion of the sleeves were strips of two-inch-wide brocaded ribbon that formed a bouffant crown over the upper arm and were secured with plain blue ribbon. Below them, the sleeve billowed out for about a foot, then was caught with another blue ribbon at the wrist, finally cascading in a shower of white lace over the hand.

The practice of covering one's head at all times having gone out with the Tudors, Judith would wear a simple veil of white lace affixed to a skull cap.

It was a beautiful dress, and Judith knew she would be proud to wear it.

When she was not sewing, Judith was questioning every woman she could corner, from her mother and sister down to the humblest serving woman, about sex. She had started her courses only a year before and knew only that these were something women had and that having them meant she was actually a woman. Frightened by what she heard, her head filled with many facts and much fiction and superstition, Judith had to keep reminding herself how gentle and loving Richard was in order not to call the whole thing off.

Finally, after the wedding banns had been read in both her and Richard's parish churches for three consecutive weeks and all the sewing and other preparations were completed, the morning of the wedding arrived. Bishop Wentworth, who was a friend of her father's, assisted by the local vicar and the vicar of Richard's parish church, performed the ceremony at the church door, as was the custom. Judith was resplendent in her white gown, with her long, dark hair flowing across her shoulders, and surrounding the skull cap on her head, a circlet set with pearls, and on her arms sprigs of rosemary tied with and trailing blue ribbons, which the young men would later pull off as wedding favors and wear in their hats.

For his part, Richard was wearing a tan-colored silk suit, the jacket fitted and belted at the waist, with a white linen collar edged with lace and silk-covered buttons. The cuffs of the jacket were also white and edged with lace. On his feet were boots of the softest fawn leather with deep asymmetrical cuffs at the knees. His shoulder-length blond hair was shiny, and his mustache and goatee were perfectly trimmed. Sir William carried the white-plumed, fawn-colored, broad-brimmed hat that Richard would put on after the ceremony.

All the guests agreed that they had seldom seen a more handsome couple.

First, copies of the wedding contracts were presented to the bishop. Next, Judith's father officially "gave her away" to Richard, a ritual accompanied by tears on the part of both Sophia and Diana. This "giving away" signified the formal granting of Judith's dowry to Richard. Judith had no idea of what her dowry consisted. She trusted her father to be generous.

Once she and Richard had exchanged their wedding promises, Richard removed the half of the gimmel ring from her finger and placed it and its other half, as well as the third which the vicar had kept, on a white velvet cushion for the bishop to bless. Next, Richard removed Lady Sophia's ring and placed it on the ring finger of Judith's right hand. Then he placed the now joined gimmel ring first on the index finger of her left hand, then on her middle finger, and finally on the ring finger, where it would stay. Her mother had explained to her that moving the ring from one finger to another would expel any demons that might want to ruin the marriage.

After the ring ceremony, the bishop said a few words, and then the two vicars had their say. Judith would not have been able to repeat one word of this triple sermon, nor could she have told what she was thinking instead. That whole part of the wedding was a blur to her.

The feast that followed was a blur as well. Receiving the guests seemed to take forever, and Judith couldn't remember what she had said or not said to anyone. She couldn't even remember who had been there. Nancy's kitchen crew had outdone themselves, and the tables groaned with beautiful food, but Judith was too excited to eat. She barely touched what was set before her and just sipped a little wine. Toast after toast followed, and although she was able to smile and clap, later she remembered nothing.

As often as was polite, her eyes went to Richard. He seemed to be totally in the moment, greeting people by name, saying exactly the right things, smiling, yet still present to her. Every few minutes, he would reach over and squeeze her hand or kiss her cheek, each time looking directly into her eyes. This is my husband, Judith kept thinking to herself. This suave, confident, handsome man is my husband. It was too much to take in.

The feast went on for hours. Judith felt herself wilting. The wine and lack of food began to tell on her, and she found herself leaning back in her chair, her eyes staring into nothing.

Richard noticed this and sent a servant to tell Diana that it was time for the "bedding." Amid many ribald comments by the guests, most of which Judith didn't understand, he led Judith to the bridal chamber, which was softly lit and filled with vases of flowers. The bed curtains were tied back with white and blue sashes, and the bed was splendid in the new sheets and coverlet that Judith would take with her to her new home. The two fathers and Richard's male friends took him into an adjoining chamber to dress him in his nightclothes, while the two mothers and the female guests did likewise with Judith. Then they were led to the bridal bed. Once they were situated in the bed, and after a final toast and cheers by all the guests and family members who had accompanied them, with kisses from their two mothers, Judith and Richard were at last alone.

Upon rising from the dining table, Judith had found herself wide-awake but still weak. As apprehensive as she was about her wedding night, she suddenly realized how hungry she was, but she was unwilling to say anything to Richard. He, however, sensed her discomfort.

"Judith, you didn't eat tonight. Aren't you hungry?" he asked.

"Well," Judith began, unsure how to respond.

"Well, I think you should eat something," Richard said, clearly amused. "I don't want you passing out on me on our wedding night!"

His levity made Judith feel better, but she said, "How can I? They've left us up here by ourselves. Will we have to go back downstairs?"

"If I'm not mistaken," said Richard, "we are well provided for." With that he pulled back the curtain and swung his legs from the bed. "Look, they've left us a veritable feast!"

Indeed, a small table had been laid with all sorts of sweetmeats and a decanter of sweet wine. "I think this was meant for afterwards," said Richard, "but let's enjoy it now."

He helped Judith into her slippers and then down from the high bed onto the floor and led her to the table, pulling out the chair so that she could sit. He poured wine for each of them and said, smiling at her, "What would you like, my beautiful wife?"

"Oh, Richard, that sounds so strange!" cried Judith.

"But good, I hope?"

"Oh, yes, of course, my gallant husband!" Judith replied, reaching over to grab his hand.

This banter helped Judith to relax, and she selected some food and ate with great enjoyment while Richard gave a running, often humorous, commentary on the wedding feast.

The food definitely made Judith feel stronger, and when they had finished their wine and Richard had led her back to bed, she was ready for whatever might happen.

Since she had no idea what to do, Judith allowed Richard to take the lead in their lovemaking, and she found that she enjoyed everything he did. His every move was gentle, and his kisses, which were so much longer and deeper than she had ever experienced, caused sensations that were entirely new to her. When he finally penetrated her, Judith thought she had never felt anything so wonderful.

Once they both lay back on their pillows, Judith turned to Richard and said, "Now that we're married, do we now get to do this anytime we want to?"

Convulsing with laughter, Richard rolled over to kiss her, saying, "Yes, my love, anytime we want. Would you like to do it again?"

"Yes, please," Judith said, "if you don't mind."

"I'll show you how much I mind," chuckled Richard.

When they awakened in the morning, the sun was midway to its zenith. While they were sleeping, someone had tiptoed in and laid out clothes for both of them. As she slid from the bed, Judith noticed spots of blood on the sheet, but she didn't worry, as she had been warned this would happen. She hoped Richard had seen it and would never have any doubt that she had come to him a virgin.

All eyes were on them as they entered the great hall of Waldby House. Their parents rushed up to them, their mothers kissing their smiling faces and their fathers shaking Richard's hand.

"Come, your guests are waiting," Diana urged, taking Judith by the hand.

The wedding feast would last for two more days, but now Judith was ready for it. All her anxieties had been dispelled by Richard's skillful lovemaking. As many of the guests remarked among themselves, Judith was glowing with happiness.

When the day of their departure for Chapman Hall came, however, Judith's fears returned. How could she leave her parents and the only home she had ever known? When would she see her brothers and sister again? How could she run a household of her own?

Everyone tried to allay those fears. Her family reminded her that they were at most three days away; the Chapmans reminded her that they would still be with her and Richard for months, as their new home was not yet built, and Sophia would teach her all about the household. Her mother told her she was a married woman now and her place was with her husband. All Richard had to do was kiss her to make her feel better.

It had been decided that Colin and Clara, who were married to each other, should accompany the newlyweds to their new home. The Chapmans would be taking their butler and their cook to their new home, and Colin would become the new butler. This was quite a step up for Colin, and both he and Clara were pleased, even if it meant leaving their families behind. Diana was unwilling to part with Nancy, but Sophia assured Judith that the cook's helper at Chapman Hall, who was good enough to make the cook jealous, would stay with the house.

Finally all was ready, with Judith's many trunks securely stowed, and all the tearful goodbyes said. The Chapmans with their valet and maid led the way, with Judith and Clara in the coach that Judith's siblings had given her as a wedding present. Richard and Colin rode beside the coaches on horseback.

The party made the same stops Judith and her mother had made when they went to visit Chapman Hall, but those stops were so different now for Judith! Each night meant Richard as a bed partner and time for them to talk and plan. The days of riding were long for Judith, but the nights made up for them.

Finally, the gracious sight of Chapman Hall appeared on the horizon. Judith thought back to her visit earlier, when she had wondered if this would indeed be her new home. That visit seemed as though it had taken place years before instead of the few months that had actually elapsed. The house looked more somber than it had in the early summer sunshine. The trees were beginning to lose their leaves, and the sky was cloudy. The north side of the house, where the circular drive was, had fewer windows than the southern exposure, and the dark stones seemed ominous.

"Poor old house," said Richard as he helped Judith to alight from the coach, "it looks so sad. It is waiting for you to brighten it up."

"It's beautiful, Richard," Judith replied. "I know I will love living here with you." And though the dark stone was still forbidding, she meant it with all of her heart.

The servants had refreshments ready for them in the same parlor where Sophia had entertained Judith and her mother before. Once they had refreshed themselves, Richard led Judith to the same room she and her mother had occupied during their visit.

"We'll sleep here while my parents are still in the house," Richard explained. "Once they have moved out, you may select the room you want. Being the only son, I get to keep the second best bed, of course, but I also get to keep the best bed. My mother wants everything new."

Then came the task of unloading the trunks and getting organized. The original part of the house, which was attached to a pele tower built in the fourteenth century, was still the main inhabited part of the house. The parlor and Sir William's study, with the guest room above them, were in a section that had been added during the sixteenth century. Once Sophia had moved in, she had decided that the house needed to be expanded in a symmetrical way, so under her guidance the house had more than doubled in size. The only part of the addition that was being used at that point, however, were some servants' quarters in the tower that formed the east end of the house and the newly designated large dining hall that formed its middle, its ceiling soaring up as high as the base of the crenellated wall that topped the sixteenth-century addition. Judith remembered that dining hall from her visit as the place where Sophia had introduced her and her mother to the neighboring gentry. It was to the unfinished parts of the house that the servants took all of Judith's baggage except the personal items that would fit in her and Richard's bedroom. Colin and Clara established themselves in one of the rooms of the new tower.

Judith was fascinated with the old tower, with its arrow slits and squared lines. Her family home was so much newer. Her great-grandfather had been a wool merchant during the reign of Queen Elizabeth, and the family home was built on land given to him by the queen (whose father, Henry VIII, had confiscated it from the Church) as repayment, along with his knighting, for money he had lent to the queen. It was built of stone as well, and had bay-window sections like Chapman Hall, but its stone was much lighter in color, and since it had been built all at once, it had the precise symmetry that Sophia had so desired but couldn't quite achieve, since she was adding onto an older building.

Judith's great-grandfather had not liked country life, preferring to be near the port and his business, and her grandfather had felt the same, but her father loved it and was happy to remain there and raise many of the sheep whose wool his father and brother then sold. After his father died, he and his brother continued the same arrangement.

Like Judith's father, Sir William Chapman preferred the country, and sheep were his passion, as they had been for his ancestors before him and promised to be for Richard.

Thus Judith was really quite at home in Chapman Hall. She already knew what went on during each of the farming seasons and how the household's activities changed. She had just never been in charge of them before, but Sophia was a good teacher, and Judith was a quick learner.

The first few weeks were taken up with visits from neighbors. Sophia arranged a reception for the newlyweds, but not everyone could attend, so several days out of the week were devoted to receiving visitors or calling on elderly gentry for whom traveling to Chapman Hall would have been difficult. Through it all, Judith came to love and respect her mother-in-law very much.

Through all the activity, Judith forgot to notice whether her courses had come, and when she finally remembered, she realized that she had not had them since before the wedding. She supposed that all the change and excitement had thrown off her system. When another month had passed, however, she spoke to Sophia about it.

Sophia was jubilant. "Oh, Judith, how wonderful! I have so looked forward to being a grandmother. I can't wait until Diana hears about it. She will be thrilled!"

"What?" Judith went pale. "You think I'm with child? I thought I was just run down from all the activity we have been having.

Really? I might be pregnant?"

"Very likely, very likely," gushed Sophia. "We'll have the midwife in tomorrow. Will you tell Richard now or wait till the midwife verifies your condition?"

"I'll wait, of course," said Judith, glad that Sophia hadn't just blurted the news out to the whole household. "I was hoping Richard and I would have some time to be alone at first, but I guess that's not meant to be."

"Well, I need to get those fellows who are building our house to hurry. You and Richard will need your privacy with a newborn, though you can be sure that William and I will do everything we can to help."

"Thank you so much, Lady Sophia. I have really come to depend on you," replied Judith truthfully. "I know nothing about having babies, much less taking care of them."

"It's the least I can do for my son's wife and my old friend's daughter, Judith, but I've come to love you as my own," said Sophia, kissing Judith's cheek. "You'll make a wonderful mother; I'm sure of it."

The midwife readily confirmed Sophia's suspicions, and Richard was ecstatic when Judith told him the news. "I knew from our wedding night that you were a lusty wench, Judith," Richard teased. Sir William's comment was that Judith would be a better producer than their best ewe.

Judith dispatched a letter to Diana, and Diana replied post-haste that she would start planning to be there with Judith when the baby came.

Judith was healthy throughout her pregnancy except for a few episodes of morning sickness, and the time passed fairly quickly for her, since she was still learning to run a house and since clothes for the baby had to be sewn. Clara, whose fingers had not yet recovered from making Judith's trousseau, was pressed into service again, and Sophia sent for a woman in the village who taught Judith and Clara how to adorn the baby clothes with beautiful embroidery and cutout patterns.

Sophia insisted that Judith and Richard move into the room where she had lain in when she had Richard. It was much larger than the guest room and had room for a cradle. It housed the "second-best bed," which was always handed down to the oldest son. "William inherited that bed from his father, who got it from his, and so on, Judith," Sophia informed. "Now it will be Richard's, as it should be."

The bed was lovely, made of carved dark wood and draped with emerald green silk. Judith noticed that a wooden cradle already lay beside the bed. "Was that Richard's crib?" she asked, and Sophia replied that it was. "I am so happy that I have lived to see another baby use that crib. My uncle, Charles Penhurst, had it made for me when I was expecting Richard. I hope you don't mind using a hand-me-down," said Sophia. Judith, of course, was delighted to use it.

The room had a large window facing the south, and it had a rarity outside of royal palaces, a graderobe, or privy, set into the corner of the old tower. A heavy curtain covered its entrance, and a wooden seat covered the hole in the stone.

"I'll have someone clean it out before you move in," assured Sophia.

"How can it be cleaned?" inquired Judith. "Does someone have to go down there?"

"Oh, no," chuckled Sophia. "That would be asking too much even from the lowliest servant. There's a door at the bottom of the tower. They rake out the contents and put in new straw and fragrant grasses. I find that it helps to keep the smell down if you keep some cedar chips on the windowsill. Do hang your woolens in there, though. Moths hate the smell even more than we do," Sophia laughed.

"I will definitely follow that advice," said Judith.

The switch of rooms was accomplished quickly, with Clara and

Sophia's maid doing most of the work. Sophia was not unhappy to have all their belongings put into trunks and transported to the guest room. "It will be one less thing for me to see about when our new house is ready," she cooed. "Oh, I will be so glad to be in a smaller place! William and Richard and I have been rattling around in this house for so many years. I thought I wanted a grand mansion, but now that I'm getting old, it's just too much trouble. Now you and Richard can finally fill it up with young ones!"

For her part, Judith was glad to be able to empty her trunks permanently. With the baby on the way, traipsing to the other side of the house and up and down stairs every time she needed something was becoming more and more difficult.

The only pall on Judith's happiness was the increasingly alarming news from London. The king had once again issued a writ demanding "ship money," not just from the inhabitants of coastal England whose homes might need naval defense, but from all areas. Not only did the people, already overburdened with other taxes, not want to pay the tax, but many saw this move by Charles, which he pursued without the consent of Parliament (which he had dissolved), as an attempt to dispense permanently with parliamentary government.

For the Waldby and Chapman families, whose livelihood depended on the wool trade, such taxation was especially onerous and would be even more so if the king went after the port cities that refused to pay the tax as they had previously. Both families were staunch supporters of the monarchy, but they were not blind to the restraint that Parliament helpfully exercised over the king's schemes. Previously, little money from this tax had actually been collected, but this time, with the Scots' objecting to Charles's attempt to install bishops in the Church of Scotland, people were afraid a war between England and Scotland would break out and Charles would try harder to enforce his writ. There was little else in the conversation of Richard and his father, and the letters from Judith's father were even more alarming.

By the time Judith was ready to deliver, the elder Chapmans' new house was complete, and they had vacated the guest room to make room for Diana. Sir Henry, like Richard and Sir William, was busy with farming chores and could not leave.

Judith began having contractions during the night, and Colin was sent to the village to bring back the midwife. Judith had never been present for a birth, since she was considered still too young to be in attendance when her sister had given birth, and she had been only a toddler herself when Stephen was born. While the midwife was being fetched, Richard dressed himself but lay down beside Judith, letting her squeeze his hand each time a contraction came.

The midwife arrived all a-bustle, with her bag bearing the tools of her trade and a stool on which she could sit beside the laboring woman. She insisted that the bed be draped with many layers of clean linen and that the room be darkened, lit by only a single rush light, and she dismissed Richard from the room, allowing only Diana and Clara to remain. Richard spent a sleepless night upstairs in the solar, trying in vain to concentrate on his farm accounting. When the sun came up, he checked on Judith, and when told that her labor would continue, he headed out to the fields to clear his head.

As soon as she had the room the way she wanted it, the midwife set about rubbing Judith's belly and private parts with oil of lilies, and soon the room smelled wonderful. As the contractions got stronger, she made Judith get up and walk around each time one started. Judith had to admit that the contractions hurt less when she was standing up. Eventually, however, during one of these contractions, her water broke, and after that, the midwife confined her to bed. Diana and Clara plied her with soup to keep up her strength, but when she reached the transition stage, when some muscles were pulling up while others were pushing down, she wanted nothing but to get it all over with. For a brief moment, she cursed Richard, her mother, the midwife, and even God.

Finally, in the late morning of June 6, 1637, Stuart Waldby

Chapman came into the world, crying lustily as the coolness hit his formerly warm body. The midwife, mumbling prayers for mother and baby the whole time, cut the umbilical cord, extracted the placenta, and sent Clara out to bury both. She then dressed the navel with an astringent powder of aloes and frankincense and bathed the baby in warm water with milk and sweet butter added. Finally, she anointed the baby's body with oil of acorns, bound the navel with strips of cloth, and swaddled him. Diana made sure to place a sixpence on his buttocks under the swaddling clothes to keep the devil away.

Once the baby was swaddled and Clara and Diana had cleaned Judith and changed the bedclothes, the midwife placed the baby on Judith's left side, near her heart. Judith almost burst with happiness, all pain now forgotten.

By this time, Richard had returned from the fields. After he had kissed and congratulated Judith, the midwife handed him his son, intoning the age-old formula, "Father, see, there is your child. God give you much joy with it, or take it speedily to His bliss." Richard was a bit taken aback by the latter choice but made the resolution and said a prayer then and there that his son would live a long and safe life.

Colin was soon dispatched to ride to the elder Chapmans with the news, and once the baby had suckled for the first time and Judith had fallen asleep, Diana penned a letter to Sir Henry to be sent out the next day, urging him, along with Sally and Alex, who were to be the baby's godparents, to come as soon as possible.

Although the midwife had located two women willing to act as wet nurses for the newcomer, Judith chose to feed him herself. "I'm not going anywhere, so why not?" she replied when Diana insisted that nursing one's own child just wasn't done among the gentry.

"Judith, you are incorrigible!" remonstrated Diana, but Judith held firm.

"Nancy told me that if a baby nurses from another woman, he may take in that woman's evil. She also said that nursing her babies had helped her get her figure back sooner," said Judith.

"Nancy—my cook?" replied Diana, amazed. "You plan on taking the advice of a cook?"

"Well, she does have healthy children, you have to admit," said Judith. "And a really good figure, even though she's given birth eight times."

"Yes, but," began Diana.

"No 'but' about it," said Judith. "He's my baby, and I'm going to feed him myself."

"All right. I give up," said Diana. "You'll do what you want no matter what I say. You always have."

"Not true," giggled Judith. "You wanted me to marry Richard, and I did."

"That was different," said Diana. "You wanted that even more than I did."

"Well, that's so," acknowledged Judith.

As was customary, for the first three days Judith was kept in a dark, quiet room. She was fed mostly liquids, both to keep up her strength and to help her produce milk. Several times a day, under the midwife's instructions, Clara applied plasters, dressings, ointments, and salves to stop bleeding and reduce inflammation. After she was allowed to sit up, she still remained in the room, with Stuart's cradle right beside her and Clara sleeping on a pallet on the floor. Richard would sleep in the solar for forty days after the birth, as was the custom.

During her lying-in period, she had lots of visitors from the neighboring gentry. So many women died following childbirth that people came to visit quickly, in case it was their last time to see the mother. Fortunately, Judith was young and healthy, and those "gossips" were joyful rather than sad visits.

Within two weeks, the Waldby clad arrived for the baptism. The midwife carried the baby into the church on a cushion. When asked by the vicar, Richard replied that the baby's name was Stuart

Waldby Chapman. The godparents, Sally and Alex, promised that they would raise the child in case his parents could not, and would bring him up to be a good Christian.

A feast followed at Chapman Hall. The large table in the dining room groaned under sweet wheat biscuits, marmalade, and "marchpane," with sweet wine and mead for all. Guests brought lovely gifts. Judith had to miss it all, of course, as her lying-in period was not yet over, but she received glowing accounts from all who attended and was able to enjoy some of the goodies later. Because of her condition, Richard did not share with her the topic of conversation among the men of the family, who were appalled over the king's treatment of three gentlemen who had dared to write pamphlets criticizing the king's choice for Archbishop of Canterbury, William Laud. These worthies had had their ears cut off, and Richard and most others among the gentry were worried that Parliamentary anger would boil over, especially in West Yorkshire, where supporters of Parliament were numerous.

Baby Stuart, named out of loyalty to King Charles, grew to be a healthy toddler. Judith nursed him for a year, at which time he insisted on drinking instead only from the silver cup that his godparents had given him. Judith settled into the rhythm of the house, and she and Richard were very happy. The fields were producing well: sheep, cattle, oats, barley, and flax filled every inch, and they were able to sell more than enough wool to Judith's uncle to buy the fine wheat flour that they kept for special treats, as well as beautiful silks and other fabrics for their clothing. The farming people attached to the estate were happy, too, as Richard was generous with them and demanded only what was fair. Under his father's tutelage, Richard had become the perfect gentleman farmer.

When Stuart was a year old, Judith began the task of decorating those parts of the house that Sophia had not begun. Since the kitchen and cold kitchen in the old section were more than adequate for the whole house, she decided she would turn the eastern third of the house into guest rooms and sitting rooms, following the plan that Sophia had outlined. She brought in carpenters to begin the task of lining the walls with paneling to keep out the cold, and she and Richard rode into Bradford to buy mats woven of rushes to cover the stones of the ground floor and to select woolen rugs for the wood-plank floors of the upper two levels.

Unlike the rooms on the west side of the house, which had no clearly demarcated levels and were connected by partial, doorless stairways that seemed to have grown accidentally as they were needed, the floors in the east addition, under Sophia's direction, had been made with full stairways, hallways, and doors that closed. To get from the western parts of the house to the eastern, one must either cross the large dining hall on the ground floor or follow the balcony that looked down upon the dining hall from many feet up. This gave the dining room the feeling of being enormous, even though it was only about thirty feet by thirty feet, and it provided both the family and their guests with privacy. Judith was impressed by Sophia's foresight.

When Sophia and Sir William had vacated the main rooms in the west side of the house, Colin and Clara had moved into the servants' quarters on the third story of the old tower, and their rooms in the east tower were given to the elder Chapmans' servants. Now that the elder Chapmans had departed, those quarters would be used for the servants of guests.

Judith was eager to complete the task of furnishing the eastern section of the house, as the stream of visitors who had been coming to see the new baby, many from too far away not to stay over at least one night, had seriously strained the house's resources to lodge them.

That task had to be postponed once again, however, when Judith became pregnant a second time. Although she was healthy throughout, and had less morning sickness than she had had with Stuart, she quickly found climbing up and down stairs difficult, and her swollen feet and ankles during the final months of the pregnancy required her to sit often with her feet up. In addition, chasing after Stuart, who could now walk, was exhausting, but she would trust his care to no one else.

Her second delivery went off as smoothly as the first, as did her lying in. Diana was with her as before, and her Waldby relatives all came for the christening. On the second Sunday of April, in 1639, Benjamin Penhurst Chapman dedicated himself to God for the first time, assisted by his godparents, Judith's brother Geoff and Richard's cousin, Mary Chapman, whom Judith had met on her first trip to Chapman Hall.

Geoff had heeded the call of the king and was about to leave for the Scottish border to join the king's army to invade Scotland and quell the rebellion caused by the king's insistence that the Scots accept the High Anglican version of the Book of Common Prayer. Geoff was sanguine about the outcome of this campaign, believing the Scots incapable of mounting a defense that was anywhere near a match for the English.

He couldn't have been more wrong, and by June the king was forced to sign the Treaty of Berwick, giving the Scots control over their own church affairs, although, as subsequent events showed, he had no intention of abiding by it.

Judith was unaware of all of this, but she noticed that Richard was much less relaxed than before. She wondered if being father of two was overwhelming him, but she hesitated to draw him out about it, preferring not to know rather than finding out that marriage and fatherhood were hard on him, not what he had bargained for.

In late June, when Geoff came for a visit, ostensibly to see his new godson, Richard at first seemed relieved but then was tenser than ever. Nevertheless, for Judith, Geoff's visit was a breath of fresh air, and she delighted in showing him her two beautiful sons and enjoying the summer weather with him and Richard.

Fall of 1639 was uneventful. Benjy was still nursing, so Judith was pretty well tied to the house. Richard was busy with the harvest, which was again a good one, though he sometimes complained that the workers he hired were becoming sullen, a departure from their behavior in the past. When Judith asked him if he knew why, he said he supposed they were mostly Parliamentary sympathizers, who resented having to work for a supporter of the king but needed to accept whatever work they could find.

"Why on earth would they not support the king?" asked Judith, incredulous. "Surely the king has been nothing but good to them!"

"You and I think so, Judith," replied Richard, "but many of the leaders in Parliament think that the king wants to put us back in the Roman Church, and they don't like it."

"Papists? Of course not! My mother has often told me about how hard Good Queen Bess worked to make sure that never happened. She even had to execute her own cousin, for goodness sake!"

"Yes," said Richard, "but Charles's queen is a French Catholic. There are those who fear her influence over him is too great."

"Do you, Richard? Do our fathers? Asked Judith, alarmed. "I don't want to be a Papist! My mother told so many stories about them and their strange ways!"

"So did mine, Judith," said Richard. "I often wondered if any of them were true. In any case, I don't think there are many people on this island who want to be Papists again, and if the king should try to push people in that direction again, there could be trouble."

"Trouble? What kind of trouble?

"From what I hear, some in Parliament are already planning to rebel against the king. Especially after he tried to force the Scots to accept religious ideas they didn't want," said Richard

"He did? When?"

"Why, just now. Geoff just came back," said Richard.

"Geoff? What did he have to do with it?" cried Judith.

Her obvious alarm reminded Richard that she had not known what was happening, so he explained everything to her.

When he had finished, she was silent for a few moments, then said, "So that's what has been bothering you. Here I was thinking that there was something wrong with me, that I no longer pleased you."

"Of course not, Judith!" assured Richard. "It's because I love you and our life together, and our sons, that I worry so much."

"But what could happen to us? We're so far away from the court, and even Scotland is far to the north of us."

"I'm afraid this religion thing is going to tear this country apart, Judith. Many people have religious ideas that are far more non-papist than ours, and if they think the king might force them to become papists, I don't know what they'll do. There are also the king's demands on Parliament. He always wants more money, and our taxes are already so high. Even though we are far inland, we have to pay that "ship money" every year, and then we pay it again indirectly when our wool goes to port. Pretty soon we'll be squeezed as dry as a turnip."

"Richard, surely we would never desert the king!"

"Of course not. Our families owe too much to the monarchy and have done for centuries. But what will we have to do to demonstrate that loyalty? That's what worries me. Geoff has already put his life in danger in a failed campaign. What will be next?"

"Oh, Richard, this makes me so sad—and so frightened! I love our life here at Chapman Hall! We cannot let anything change it! And I don't want my brother going off to fight. He could be hurt, or killed!"

"My beautiful, sweet, innocent Judith! That is my earnest wish as well. Let's keep that as our goal and cherish every minute!" He took her in his arms and held her for a long time, then kissed her tenderly and took his leave. She thought she saw a tear glisten on his cheek as he walked away.

From this time on, though she tried to put a good face on it, Judith was troubled. Whereas before she had made no attempt to keep up with the news from London, or anywhere else, except what concerned the latest fashions, now she was all ears when someone came with information about the greater world. Often she did not understand, but Richard was patient about explaining what the news meant. The shadow of the looming conflict was like a dark cloud over their happiness.

Part III

As 1639 melted into 1640, more and more bad news continued to arrive. Richard tried to keep Judith abreast of what was happening, but he never admitted how worried he was. He had begun to talk seriously with his neighbors, and he was more and more of the opinion that the king was wrong in the way he was treating his subjects and letting his ministers treat them. However, his father would hear nothing of it. Sir William was loyal to a fault, it seemed to Richard. Nevertheless, Richard knew he would not betray his father, no matter how much his conscience told him the king's detractors were right. He saw nothing but pain and heartache in his country's future, and in his own as well.

Then, as the summer wore on, the Scots rebelled again against the changes to their church mandated by Archbishop Laud, the king's appointed Archbishop of Canterbury and therefore de facto head of the English Church. Geoff stopped by on his way to the border, more sobered this time by the defeat the Scots had previously dealt the English army and much less sanguine of success. This time Judith was aware of where he was going and wept for a week after his departure, so afraid that he would be harmed.

As anticipated, the battle did not go well for the English, who were forced to slink home in defeat a second time. Geoff was slightly wounded but not immobilized. He was able to pay them a return visit on his way home, and Judith fussed over him like a mother hen.

"Geoff, I order you never to do anything like this again! It is too dangerous," she admonished him as she changed the dressing on his arm.

Geoff roared with laughter. "Judith, this was nothing. I've gotten hurt worse just playing around in the woods when I was a boy!"

"But you're no longer a boy! You should have better sense now," Judith insisted.

"Judith, when the king calls, it's a gentleman's obligation to go to his aid. Would you have our father go in my stead?"

"What? Of course not! I don't want any of you in any wars,"

Judith insisted.

"Well, if Parliament and those who support it continue to oppose the king, all of us men may have to go to his defense—Stephen, Alex, even Richard."

Judith went pale. "No! Don't even joke about that, Geoff. That's cruel."

"Judith, I'm not joking. Naturally, I'd prefer that everything be settled peacefully, but we all have an obligation to our king. We have to go when he needs us."

"But Geoff, Stephen is a child, and Alex and Richard know nothing about fighting in wars. They're farmers. The king cannot expect them to go!"

"Judith, Stephen is twenty now. He's not a child. And he has been training for war almost since you left. He would like nothing better than to be called to battle. He almost came with me this time, but I persuaded him to wait for one we were likely to win. The Scots are just too tough for us."

"No! No! No!' screamed Judith. "Don't tell me these horrible things, Geoff. They cannot be true!"

At just that point, Richard came in from the fields.

"What cannot be true, Judith?" he asked.

"Richard, Geoff says there may be more battles, and he will have to be in them—and Stephen, too, and even you and Alex. That's not true, is it?"

Richard frowned and glared at Geoff. "Yes, Judith, I'm afraid it is true. I was hoping to spare your knowing and worrying about it until it actually came to pass, hoping that this horrible conflict would be resolved before any more battles had to be fought."

"But Richard, you don't know anything about fighting a war! You'll be killed!"

"Of course I won't," assured Richard. "If I have to go, I will be in the cavalry. I have been riding since I was three, and I'm the best shot in the riding. I'll be fine."

Judith was not so easily reassured. She ranted and raved

throughout the rest of Geoff's visit. After he left, she hounded Richard incessantly for news from London and nagged him about practicing his marksmanship.

For his part, this latest defeat made Richard even more worried. After talking with various people at the wool market in Bradford, and with the village vicar, he liked even less than before what he was hearing.

Apparently William Laud, the Archbishop of Canterbury, had been pushing the English Church, with the king's permission and encouragement, closer and closer to Papism by insisting on ridiculous conformity measures in all churches. The vicar said that he and the other vicars of the area were terrified of committing some breach of etiquette that would bring down on them the wrath of the archbishop. Some clergy who had been recalcitrant had lost their parishes and with them their livings. Richard was sure that this would not end well.

The information that Geoff had brought back from Scotland was just as disturbing. The king was a Scot himself. If he couldn't keep his own people under control, how could Englishmen support him? The war had been the result of the Scots' refusal to abide by Laud's rules, and the Scots had prevailed against the king yet again, in part because the Irish troops promised to the king by fellow Yorkshireman Thomas Wentworth, Earl of Strafford, who had been appointed Lord Deputy of Ireland by the king, had not arrived in time. Geoff said that they probably wouldn't have been useful anyway. He had heard from a soldier who had been in Ireland training troops for a previous conflict that the Irish were in the army only because Wentworth forced them to be and that they were most inept pupils.

Richard had also been speaking with some of his neighbors among the gentry, many of whom were abandoning their allegiance to the king because of his financial and religious demands and because they were dismayed by his repeated dissolutions of Parliament. When asked if he would stand with the king or with Parliament,

Richard hedged.

"I have been given all I have by my father. I will abide by his counsel," he replied.

The very next day, a conversation with his father solidified a feeling of unease that he could not shake. When he broached all of his concerns to his father, Sir William was dismissive.

"Son, you're worrying for nothing," Sir William reassured. "Charles is weak, especially compared to her majesty, and even to his father, but he is not a fool. I have heard that there are already rumors of Laud's losing favor. The king will not let this thing grow into a significant conflict. You'll see."

"But what if you're wrong, Father?" insisted Richard. "He has already lost the respect and allegiance of most of our neighbors. What if they turn against us for supporting him?"

"Not support the king? Don't be a fool, boy. Our neighbors will be on their knees to the king and glad to do it, too, I'll warrant. The king is God's appointed ruler. That fellow Pym and his rabble rousers may get a few concessions from him, as others did in the time of King John, but God will protect the king's right to rule, and our neighbors would do well to remember that when they're making such treasonous statements."

"Well, I agree with them that the king is violating the terms of the Great Charter itself in not letting Parliament do its job. I can see why they're disenchanted with him."

"Richard, not you, too, surely! The Chapmans are the king's men—always have been, always will be. Don't you forget that! If these fools get out of hand, we will raise our hands to defend our king!"

Richard could see that further remonstrance was useless, so he kept silent after that, but in his heart anger and frustration were growing.

He was angry with the king for letting people like Laud and Wentworth, who were so oblivious of the consequences of their actions (or too power-hungry to care), run the country. He was angry with his father for clinging so tenaciously to a worldview that, as far as Richard could see, was on its way out.

He was also terrified of what would happen if war broke out between the king and the supporters of Parliament as it had between the king and the Scots.

His bravado in the face of Judith's hysteria had been purely an act. He knew he was no soldier. Yes, he could ride and shoot, but shooting rabbits and deer, and even wild boars, was very different from shooting human beings. What if he completely lost his courage and ran from the battlefield?

Worse still, what might happen to Judith and the boys, and his parents, while he was away? Would supporters of Parliament come and kill them and take over his home while he was not there to protect them? He knew his neighbors, who were gentlemen, would never order such a thing, but what about their soldiers and the mercenaries they might hire? Would all his crops be stolen and his animals slaughtered to provide food for a hungry army? What would it cost to outfit himself for war? Where would he get the money? What if war caused trade to dry up and he couldn't sell his wool and barley? Where would he find someone to lead his men? He knew he wouldn't be expected to lead them himself. Even Geoff, who had been a soldier for years, had hired a captain who had experience in the European wars. Where would he get soldiers? Most of the gentry who assembled troops drew from their own peasants and villagers, but he knew all too well that the ones who worked the Chapman estate had no love for the king and his ministers, with whose oppressive measures they contended daily.

Then there was the growing discontent of his neighbors. Every time he went into Bradford to the wool market, all the talk was of the conflict. If these men, whom he had known all his life, persisted in opposing the king, and if war did break out, would he have to face them across a battlefield? It was too horrible to consider.

These growing concerns obsessed Richard. His naturally cheerful disposition gave way to a seriousness and somberness that he could not avoid. He wracked his brain trying to think of a way out, but none presented itself.

He acceded to Judith's wishes and practiced his marksmanship regularly, especially working on reloading his musket and pistol as quickly as possible. He set up an obstacle course on which to practice making quick moves on horseback and jumping his horse over barriers. He even began teaching Stuart, who was only three, how to ride. Stuart took to it immediately and begged his father daily to let him practice. Richard loved being with him, but he recoiled at the thought that he might be training his firstborn son only to become cannon fodder.

Some hope seemed to appear later in 1640, when Parliament, in the session that became known as the Long Parliament, accused Laud of treason and confined him to the Tower of London, where he would remain for almost five more years. Richard hoped that with Laud no longer in charge of the church, the animosity toward the king would abate. It was not to be.

In fact, Parliament was so outraged that Thomas Wentworth had persuaded the king to dissolve the previous Parliament (because Irish troops were coming to his aid against the Scots, and he wouldn't need Parliament to pay for them), that Wentworth became their next target. John Pym led Parliament to impeach Wentworth on the basis of an accusation that he had advised the king to use the Irish army against his English opponents as well as against the Scots. At his trial, Wentworth defended himself well, and Parliament was unable to prove its case against him. Nevertheless, by using an archaic option called a Bill of Attainder, Parliament was finally able to gain the king's consent against Wentworth, and Wentworth was beheaded on Tower Hill in May of 1641.

Wentworth had been one of the king's most trusted ministers, and his fall from grace unnerved Richard even further. If this could happen to as powerful a man as Wentworth had been, what hope did he (a minor landowner compared to many) have against the power of Pym? Would it matter a whit that the Chapman family had owned their estate since the Norman Conquest? Richard was doubtful.

All the news coming out of London was bad for the king. Parliament continued to strip powers from the king until, early in 1642, it effectively ejected him from London completely.

In April of 1642, Geoff sent word that the king had set up his court at York and was looking to recruit an army to oust Parliament from London.

"Now's your chance to see some real action, Richard," Geoff's letter read. "You'll see that fighting is much more exciting than farming."

Richard's worst nightmare was coming true. He knew that it was his duty to go to the king, but everything in his being protested against it.

He put it off as long as he could, reasoning that he had to get the lambing finished and the crops sown so that the estate could run in his absence. And he didn't tell Judith.

Sir William, for his part, was ridiculously sanguine about the whole thing. Although Sir William was not that old, Richard was ready to believe his father was going senile, so oblivious did he seem to the danger facing his whole family.

When he finally told Judith, she was devastated.

"I'm going to lose you. I know it," she wailed. "These stupid wars will be the end of us."

"They won't, Judith," pleaded Richard. "You'll see. In any case, I'm just going to York, not into battle. I will offer my services to the king, but maybe since I'm so inexperienced, he will prefer that I stay here and raise food to feed the men who are actually warriors, like Geoff."

"Do you really think that could happen?" asked Judith hopefully. "Would the king be that sensible?"

"Well, why not? Someone has to feed all those people," said Richard, sounding much more positive than he felt.

"But what if the king doesn't want you to do that? What then?"

continued Judith.

"Judith, we'll cross that bridge when we get to it. I'm not able to see into the future," said Richard. "Please don't make this harder than it is."

"All right," said Judith, putting her arms around him, "but who is going to take care of this place while you're gone? I have no idea how to conduct farming chores or make farming decisions."

"I have given extra authority to Giles for that purpose," assured Richard, "and my father will come several times a week to make sure all is well."

"Thank God we have him," said Judith. "And what does your mother think of all this?"

"She feels as you do; she's worried how it will come out, but having been through much upheaval in her youth, she's more philosophical about it than young ones like us can be, we who have known nothing but peace all our lives."

By the time Richard finally reached York, the king was already planning to remove his court to Nottingham.

Geoff used his influence as a veteran of the Scottish wars to get an audience with the king for Richard. As Richard waited for his turn at the entrance to Charles's throne room, he was struck by how small and insignificant the king looked, seated in a chair that had been made for Henry VIII. To think that on this man's whim hung the lives and livelihoods of so many! It made Richard ill to think of it.

When his turn did come, Richard found Charles to be pleasant but understandably distracted.

"Yes, yes, I've heard of your father. A loyal subject. Wish they were all so. Are you here to volunteer for the northern army?" said the king.

"I'm here to serve you in any way I can, Sire," replied Richard. "I would be happy to provide a certain amount of food for the army from my estate, if that would please your highness."

"That's nice, boy, but what I really need is regiments," said the king. "Can you outfit a regiment?"

"I don't know," said Richard, totally confounded. "I had not thought about that. Maybe I can. Maybe Geoff can help me."

"Geoff who?" asked the king.

"Geoff Waldby, Sire, my brother-in-law," said Richard.

"Oh, yes, good man, that. Do it, then," said the king, looking away to see who the next caller was.

Richard was beside himself. A regiment! That meant hundreds of men! Where would he get the money? Men needed to be paid for their services, and they needed food, clothing, armor, weapons— all the accouterments of an army. He didn't even know what those were, much less how to get them.

When he told Geoff, though, Geoff was thrilled. "Damn, Richard, that'll be great! Don't worry. I'll help you get started. I know just the man for you."

The very next day, Geoff took Richard to meet a man called Andrew Selden, the man who had outfitted Geoff's own troop.

Selden was only too happy to do business once he found out that Richard was the only heir to Chapman Hall and its lands. He had ridden through West Yorkshire on occasion and had noted the quality of the land and its sheep and crops—not a bad take, he said, if Richard should default on the loan. He undertook to provide everything Richard needed, including the soldiers and the captain.

Richard didn't like Selden at all. Although Selden had the air of a gentleman, Richard didn't trust him. When he looked into Selden's eyes, he saw only icy calculation, no warmth. Geoff, however, was full of confidence.

"Richard, he offers the best terms of anyone, and he delivers what he promises. What more can you ask?"

Richard had to agree that the first impression a person made didn't necessarily indicate what he was inside. He agreed to Selden's terms, and several days later when Selden came around to his lodgings, he signed the paperwork.

He committed himself to outfitting a horse regiment of a hundred men. Selden would find someone to train and lead it and would provide all the required equipment. He would also undertake keeping the soldiers paid for their services. Richard committed himself to reimbursing Selden for whatever funds were required, and he pledged Chapman Hall and its property as surety.

"Now, Richard," said Selden, addressing Richard as an equal, which, despite his gentlemanly clothing and speech, Richard resented. "A regiment cannot be assembled overnight. I suggest you go home to your wife and family and take care of your estate. I will notify you when everything is ready."

As there was nothing more to be done, Richard complied, much to Judith's delight, although the thought of a regiment filled her with apprehension. At least she could be happy for the time being.

In the months that ensued, Geoff followed the king to Nottingham, where he trained with his men while the king tried to negotiate with Parliament. When that failed, he accompanied the king into Wales, helping to recruit Welshmen into the king's army. The Welsh were fierce fighters, like the Scots, and thus would be welcome additions to the royal army if they could be persuaded to stay on task and not wander off when the going got rough. The Welsh had little loyalty to the English after all the futile years of struggling for their independence, and they could not be trusted too far. Nevertheless, with some of the most capable military men in the kingdom having gone over to Parliament's side, the king could not be choosy.

While he was still waiting for word from Selden, Richard got the news that a party of royalist supporters had tried to burn down buildings outside the port city of Hull in East Yorkshire but that they had been driven back by gunfire from those who defended the port. Richard wondered if any of the buildings belonged to Judith's uncle and whether, if they did, Judith's family would switch its allegiance.

Whenever his farm tasks allowed, Richard trained, as well as he knew how, for the possibility of battle. The vicar had some books on wars of the past, and Richard read them voraciously. Although he knew that warfare had changed considerably since the religious wars on the Continent covered by the books, he figured any knowledge was better than none. Ignorance of what to expect in battle could well cost him his life. Selden had told him that each member of the regiment would receive a sword and two pistols, so Richard practiced his shooting and hacked at bales of hay with a sword that his father had had in his youth.

The latter activity greatly amused Stuart, who demanded a bale of hay that he could hack with the tiny wooden sword Colin had carved for him. His obvious delight was alarming to Richard, but spending time with his son was so important to him that he allowed Stuart to hack to his heart's content. By this time Benjy, who had turned three, was ready to learn to ride, so the three of them spent numerous happy hours in the saddle touring the Chapman fields. If the war hadn't been like a devil just over his shoulder, Richard would have cherished this time with his boys as among the best times of his life.

The next news that came was that the royal army had confronted the Parliamentary army at Edgehill, in Warwickshire, trying to take back London. The battle had proven inconclusive because the king had chosen to repair to Oxford to regroup. It was time for Richard to go to his aid, but how could he without a regiment?

Finally, at the beginning of November, Colin came into Richard's study to tell him he had a visitor.

The visitor introduced himself as Captain Brian Johnson. He had fought in the battle of Edgehill and was able to give Richard the comforting news that though Geoff had again been wounded, this time in the leg, his wound was not fatal, and he had been taken back to Waldby House to recuperate.

The Captain's other news was that he had been engaged by Andrew Selden to take command of Richard's newly formed regiment. He told Richard he had fought in the Low Countries and in western France, as well as against the Scots, and he felt confident that he could build an effective fighting force for Richard to take into the king's service. He had already contacted a number of men who had fought beside him in those conflicts, and they had signed on.

Captain Johnson was a bear of a man, as tall as Richard but much stockier. The muscles of his arms strained at the fabric of his doublet. Richard could imagine how much damage a hack from this man could do to an enemy. This, along with the man's self-assurance and apparent competence made Richard feel better. He confessed to the captain his own lack of experience, but the captain made light of it.

"I've rarely seen a gentleman who couldn't ride and shoot, Sir. All you'll need is a bit of understanding of how a regiment works as a unit," assured the captain. "If you can run a place like what I see here, you can certainly fight in a battle."

Richard wasn't so sure it would be that easy, but he forbore saying so and thanked the captain for his kind words.

They agreed that Richard would meet the new regiment just after the new year began and train with them at Oxford.

The holidays of 1642 were happy times for Richard's sons. Benjy was just old enough to appreciate the small gifts from Father Christmas, and Stuart was delighted with the new pony and saddle that were now his. With a house full of sweetmeats and fall fruits and nuts, the boys were oblivious to the strained looks on their parents' faces. For all Richard and Judith knew, this could be their last time together as a family.

The new year dawned chilly and cloudy, befitting Richard's somber mood. On January 2, he had to acknowledge that there was no help for it. He had to go. With no idea what to expect, he packed his things, bade a tearful goodbye to his parents, his sons, and Judith, and set off for Oxford.

Even as a lone horseman, he had to ride nine days before reaching the vicinity of Oxford. As he rode, the countryside seemed deserted. He tried to tell himself that people were still at home celebrating, but much of the area through which he passed was Parliamentary country, where people probably didn't even celebrate, believing the old Yule customs to be pagan and Papist. A more likely explanation was that the men were either already training or were, like him, en route to their training locations.

The city of Oxford was surrounded with military encampments. It looked to Richard as though everyone on the island of Britain was living in a tent. It took him the better part of a day to locate Captain Johnson.

After the usual pleasantries, the captain showed Richard to his tent, which was surprisingly nice in its amenities, as befitted the owner of the regiment. After he had put down his belongings, Richard accompanied the captain around the camp to meet his men. As the day's drilling had taken place in the morning, between daybreak and noon, the men were at liberty. Many were in the process of building their evening fires; some had walked into the city to visit taverns or brothels, bored with just sitting around.

The first of his soldiers Richard met was a very young man named Jeremy Fletcher. Captain Johnson noticed the surprised look on Richard's face when he was introduced. Although Jeremy was rather tall, almost as tall as Richard, he was very slender and wiry, with dusty hair and green eyes, and he had just the beginnings of a beard sprouting on his chin. He looked much too young to be a soldier.

"Don't let his looks fool you, Sir. He may be young, but Jeremy is a seasoned veteran. We fought together in Scotland, and you won't find a more capable man on a horse. He also has the eye of a falcon and a truer aim with a pistol than anyone I know, including me." Johnson chuckled at this joke on himself.

"I'm so glad to meet you, Jeremy," said Richard honestly, offering his hand. "It appears you will be a valuable asset to our regiment."

"Thank you, Sir," replied Jeremy. "I will do my best to serve you well."

"You'll have a chance to test him yourself, Sir," said the captain. "I have asked Jeremy to work with you, to help you to acclimate to army life."

"Thank you, Captain," bowed Richard. "I am pleased to have such an accomplished tutor."

Richard and Jeremy began working together the next morning. At first, getting up so early was difficult for Richard. On the farm, people rose with the sun; here, everyone was expected to be dressed, fed, and on the field before the sun even peeked over the horizon. Fortunately, the winter of 1642 was mild, and snows were few.

As the days of the first week of training went by, Richard was growing more and more fatigued. Although he considered himself a hard worker, he realized that the tasks he performed on his estate were much less physically demanding than riding, shooting, and slashing. Jeremy showed him how to maneuver his horse to avoid a pikeman's thrust or a musket's bullet, how to shoot and reload his pistols quickly, how to use a sword to do maximum damage to an enemy or at least to disarm him. None of these tasks was to Richard's liking, but he knew he had to learn in order to preserve his own life. At night, when he was alone in his tent, only thoughts of the smiling faces of Judith and the boys and his parents enabled him to sleep to face another day.

One evening as they sat around the campfire, Richard asked Jeremy how he had come to be a soldier at such a young age.

Jeremy explained that he had been born on a farm in Lincolnshire, where his father had been a wheat mower. Unlike Richard, he had hated farm life and had hated his father for not giving him a better one. After one particularly bad argument with his father, he had run away. He was lucky enough to fall in with some cavalrymen on their way to Scotland to fight for the king. At first, all he was allowed to do was groom the horses, but soon he showed such skill and promise that he was allowed to become a cavalryman himself. He was only sixteen when the fighting began in Scotland.

"How did you learn so much about horses, though," asked Richard. "Most farm boys in Yorkshire don't have access to horses."

"Not in Lincolnshire, neither, Sir," replied Jeremy. "But Sir John, him that owned the property, he took a fancy to me when I was but little, and he let me tarry around the stables, and Marcus, the hostler, let me ride and taught me how to care for a horse."

"When this war, or whatever it is, is over," said Richard, "maybe you can come back to Yorkshire with me and teach my sons how to become skilled horsemen like you."

"Thank you, Sir," said Jeremy. "That's a bloody fine offer, but when this is over, I'm going to America. My sainted mother, God rest her soul, died before she could live out her dream of going there. It's my duty to do that for her."

"Well, if you change your mind, let me know," said Richard.

"I would, Sir, if I did," replied Jeremy, "but I won't. You'll teach them yourself, then, Sir. I wish my da had taught me something interesting like riding. The only good I got out of mowing is a strong sword arm."

"Well, in battle, that's not a bad thing to have," said Richard.

"I guess not," acknowledged Jeremy.

After the first week, Richard began to get accustomed to camp life. His muscles ached less, and he was able to sleep better. He got to know his men, listening to their stories and asking them questions. Most were city boys. Many had worked as grooms in urban stables and had learned to ride there. The youths of the country estates had all been recruited by the owners of the fields they worked. Richard was so glad Geoff had led him to Andrew Selden. It would have been impossible for Richard to recruit the young men who worked his fields: they were all on the side of Parliament. Richard remembered how sullen they had become. He wondered if even now some had deserted their jobs on the Chapman estate and were training in the regiments of his Parliamentary neighbors.

At first, Richard had relished the delicious food that was brought to him from the tumbrils that lumbered in daily from Oxford, but after watching his men roasting salt bacon skewered on their knives and letting the grease drip on their "biscuit," the hard bread that was the soldier's ration, he felt ashamed. Why should he eat better than they did? Wouldn't they be risking their lives and the livelihoods of their families the same as he would?

So he began to join them, especially for their mid-day meal, the largest of the day, enjoying their comments about how the drills had gone and learning from their experiences. As they toasted each other with their small beer, he remembered the first time he had seen a Bellarmine bottle, the vessel of choice of the common Englishman. He had been taken aback by the fierce face that glowered from the bottle's neck and had asked his father if that was the devil.

His father had roared with laughter. "Out of the mouths of babes!" he had cried. "Yes, son, that's the devil himself. That Italian demon has tortured more true Christians than all the other Papists put together!"

Only much later would Richard hear the whole story of that infamous Inquisitor. Now the memory of that story caused his doubts to rise again. What if the royal army did succeed, as it must if he was going to remain alive and in possession of his estate? Would the queen's Papist friends come and take over the island? Would another Bellarmine arise who would torture and kill those who refused to become Papists?

Richard was so lost in his thoughts that he did not realize for a minute that all eyes were on him.

"Sir?" said the soldier Richard knew only as Piers.

"Yes," replied Richard, startled from his unpleasant reverie.

"Sir, the men and I were just saying that we are happy to be fighting in your regiment, Sir," said Piers. "We never knew a gentleman could be so friendly."

Richard could feel himself blushing. "That's very kind of you,

Piers," he said, "of all of you. You're good men, strong men. If I have to risk my life, I'm glad I'll have all of you around me, although it would be better if none of us had to risk anything."

"Life is a risk, Sir," said the man called Tom. "My da always says that when there's a war, you'd better be in it, because there's no making a living any other way during a war."

"Your da may be right, Tom," replied Richard. "Such is the way of the world, I suppose."

The next morning, when Richard met with Captain Johnson, the captain echoed the men's sentiments.

"The men are happy with you, Sir," he said. "Not only are you paying them well, but you're working alongside them, never asking for any special treatment during the drills. The men notice that. You can be sure they'll do their best and more for you when we go into battle."

"Do you think that's likely, Captain?" asked Richard. "Do you see any chance that this business might be settled before any more blood is shed?"

"Well, that would be nice for some," said the captain, "but from what I hear, I don't think it will come to pass. Both sides are hell bent to win, and that means at least one more battle to come. Since nobody really won Edgehill, something has to settle this once and for all."

"That's what I thought you'd say," said Richard sourly.

"Don't worry, Sir," said the captain. "I know you've never been in a battle before, but you'll be fine. Jeremy has taught you well, and you have responded ably. With the soldier you've become, I wouldn't want to face you in battle."

"I'm glad to hear that," said Richard, smiling and clasping the captain's forearm.

By the end of the second week of drilling, Geoff, whose regiment was also training outside of Oxford, found Richard. He was still limping a little from his wound at Edgehill, but he was determined to train with everyone else and be in on the next battle.

When he found the area where Richard's regiment was training, Geoff did not immediately make his presence known. He watched the soldiers at their work until they stopped at noon to prepare their midday meal.

"Bravo, Richard!" cried Geoff, embracing his brother-in-law. "You'll be a soldier yet!"

"That's what Captain Johnson tells me," laughed Richard. "How are you, Geoff? How's your leg?"

"Almost as good as new," said Geoff. "It still hurts a bit when I ride, but it's getting better."

"I'm glad to hear it," said Richard. "Where is your regiment?"

"We're on the other side of the encampment, near the Earl of Newcastle's men," said Geoff. "But who is this Captain Johnson?"

"He's the man Andrew Selden hired to direct my regiment," replied Richard, "a veteran of many battles, and from what I've seen, a capable military leader. I feel fortunate to have him."

"And well you should," said Geoff approvingly. "I knew Selden would find you somebody good."

"That he has," acknowledged Richard.

They then walked over to meet the captain himself, and Richard also introduced Jeremy, praising his skill to Geoff.

Geoff joined Richard for the meal, during which Richard asked him about the raid on the port buildings.

"Was your family's property affected, Geoff? How do they feel about the attack?"

"Bloody angry that it didn't succeed," replied Geoff. "If it had, we would have been in possession of one of Parliament's biggest arsenals. How I wish I could have been there! Maybe the fools wouldn't have given up so easily!"

"Ah," said Richard. "The news we got was so sketchy, I didn't know what to believe."

"It's a crime, Richard," continued Geoff. "Those bloody fanatics are taking over Yorkshire! I hope the king decides to take action against them soon. If he doesn't, pretty soon we'll all be expected to turn Anabaptist!"

Richard could well believe that, knowing what he had observed in the west of the county. He didn't want to be a Papist, but he certainly didn't want to be forced to abandon the Anglican traditions that his family had followed since Henry VIII.

Geoff's visit and mention of Andrew Selden put Richard in mind of the fact that he must owe Selden a large amount of money, and indeed, a letter from Selden arrived the next day.

"I trust that you have found everything to your liking in the persons and equipment I have provided for your regiment," Selden wrote. "I know that as a farmer you do not have access to large amounts of money all at once, but I will expect payment of part of what you own me within the next month and each harvest season thereafter."

The letter concluded with the address of Selden's solicitor, who would receive the money on his behalf, and the amount owed. The cost was staggering. Richard knew it would take years, maybe a lifetime, to pay all of the debt, assuming that his land continued to produce as before. He immediately sent off a letter to his own solicitor, instructing him to pay whatever was left above the estimated costs to keep up the estate until the next harvest. He knew it left little cushion in case of emergency, but he could think of nothing else to do.

He didn't sleep much that night and was out of sorts when he went to drill the next day. His distraction almost caused a collision with another soldier's horse and taught him the lesson that in battle, his concentration had to be absolute.

As winter gave way to spring, Richard's regiment became a formidable fighting force. They learned to control their horses with their knees so that their hands could be busy with pistols and swords. They learned to act as a single unit rather than each man's going his own way, at his own speed. The captain had seen cavalry battles in several countries and knew that the tactics of the famous Prince Rupert, the king's nephew, could be effective or could backfire, depending on the circumstances. Accordingly, he arranged clear signals for his men by which he could direct them either to pursue a troop they had put to rout, as Rupert did, or to let the troop go and stay to attack the infantry. The regiment practiced doing both and alternating between them.

Soon it was Lent, and then Holy Week. Judith surprised Richard by arriving with Sophia and the children and her brother Stephen to spend Easter with him and Geoff. Richard thought it unwise of her to be on the road amid all the unrest in the country, but he was so glad to see all of them that he forgave her instantly.

The news she brought was good. So far they had not been bothered by the conflict, and the farming was going well. The ewes were beginning to lamb, and the fields were being readied for planting. Sophia acknowledged that Sir William was enjoying being in charge again and verifying the positive results of some of his breeding experiments.

Not wanting to worry any of them, Richard did not tell them about the huge sum of money he had sent to Andrew Selden. He hoped that the good farming news would mean he could make his next payment.

The boys were fascinated by everything in the army camp. Stuart, especially, now almost six, asked so many questions that Richard's head was spinning. He finally turned Stuart over to Jeremy for a half day. The young man seemed to have infinite patience in dealing with Stuart. Benjy was more impressed with the colors and textures of all he saw than with the military aspects. Richard wondered what his younger son would choose as an occupation when he grew up. Of course, as he was only four, it was too soon to tell. With Stuart, there was no question.

Once Easter was past and the families had left the camp, the soldiers returned to their drilling. Rumors had begun to circulate that fighting would begin soon, and in fact, in mid-April, Richard was summoned to the encampment of the Earl of Newcastle.

The earl was planning a campaign to take Yorkshire back for the king, and he was in the process of recruiting all the regiments that had Yorkshire connections. Although Richard was loath to fight, he could not stand by while others defended his property and his family. He agreed to go. Geoff's regiment would fight as well.

At the end of the first week of June, the army was ready to set out for West Yorkshire. The trip that had taken Richard nine days traveling alone took three weeks with an army of thousands and all its weaponry, baggage, and supplies. Richard's regiment was near the back of the march, so he could not see exactly where they were going, only where they were at the moment. Eventually, though, he began to recognize landmarks and to realize that they were heading to an area very near his home. This was new cause for alarm. What if the battle took place on his lands? Would his beautiful fields be destroyed? His animals killed? His family ravaged? Supposedly the Parliamentary leaders were godly men, but could they control their troops? He had not failed to notice that some of the royal troops were also undisciplined. These concerns created a battle inside of Richard. He did not want to shed blood or have his own blood shed, but he did not want his family harmed, either.

The earl's army met the Parliamentary forces led by Lord Fairfax on Adwalton Moor, just a few miles southeast of Bradford, and so close to the Chapman estate that Richard was sure his family could hear the noise of the battle. Fairfax had gotten word of the royal army's approach and had gone out to meet it, knowing that Bradford could not withstand a siege.

Unfortunately for the royalists, the moor provided a ditch to shield the Parliamentarians and was inhospitably pockmarked with coal pits that made it difficult for the cavalry to operate, and the royal army was heavier on cavalry than on infantry. When Newcastle realized that it was time to deploy his troops, he made the best of a bad situation, and Fairfax faced an army at least double the size of his own, which, in contrast, was much heavier on infantry than on cavalry.

Despite the disparity in size, Fairfax's troops did very well at first, and it looked as though he might win the day, but finally the tide turned in favor of Newcastle.

Richard's regiment was among the last to engage the enemy. As Newcastle was considering retreat, he ordered a regiment of pikemen to attack Fairfax's left flank of musketeers. Since the Parliamentary muskets at that point were unsupported by very many pikemen of their own, the charge was successful, and the musketeers began to flee. The Parliamentary cavalry, seeing itself becoming surrounded, tried to put up a fight, but Newcastle deployed cannons and his own cavalry against them.

True to their training, Richard and his soldiers charged into the Parliamentary cavalry, each line of horse discharging their pistols then wheeling to the side to leave room for another line to approach and fire. Richard acted by rote, just doing what he had been taught, trying to concentrate on the prescribed sequence of action, oblivious of the fates of those his shots might have hit. If enemy soldiers were able to get by and into his ranks, Richard and his fellow horsemen hacked at them with their swords until they could safely cut to the left and ride away.

By the time Richard's line came up again, the Parliamentarians on the left had turned tail and fled, so at the captain's order, Richard's line charged the remaining center infantry, dodging musket balls and pike thrusts and slashing sideways with their swords at the unprotected necks of the men on the ground.

There was no third time. The entire Parliamentary army was in retreat. The day was the king's. Most of Yorkshire was now in his hands. Some of the Royalists pursued the fleeing Parliamentarians, but Captain Johnson chose not to follow that course of action.

As Richard and his men regrouped, they gazed on a field strewn with the bodies of men and horses. Blood seemed to be everywhere. Richard said a silent prayer for the men who had been killed or wounded and for their families, who would be grieving for the rest of their lives.

He was later to learn that whereas the royal army had suffered very few casualties, about 500 Parliamentarians had perished. No one in Richard's regiment had been killed, though a few had superficial wounds.

With Newcastle's permission, Richard led his regiment and Geoff's to Chapman Hall to celebrate their victory.

Stuart and Sir William were just riding toward the stables on the north side of the house when a shout arose from the southeast.

"Soldiers! Coming this way! Everybody inside!"

Sir William hurried Stuart into the stable, handed the horses over to the groom, and bolted for the house, Stuart struggling to keep up with him.

"Grandfather, what's happening?" asked Stuart, alarmed by his grandfather's unaccustomed haste.

"I'm not sure, boy," replied Sir William, "but there may be danger. Run quickly to your mother and tell her soldiers are coming."

"Whose soldiers, Grandfather?" demanded Stuart, "ours or theirs?"

"Stuart, just go. We can't wait to find out. If they're Parliament men, we may need to protect ourselves."

"All right," said Stuart, catching some of his grandfather's urgency.

He bolted up the stairs to the room next to his mother's bedroom, where he found her sitting at the window, sewing, Clara by her side.

"Mother, soldiers are coming! We have to protect ourselves! I'll get my sword!"

"Stuart, what on earth?" asked Judith, thinking Stuart was just playing one of his army games. "Settle down!"

"No, Mother, it's true," insisted Stuart. "Grandfather went up to the solar to see if he could see whose soldiers they were. They might be our enemies coming to fight us!"

The mention of Sir William gave an air of credence to Stuart's outburst, so after sending Clara to find Benjy, who had been playing on the south terrace, Judith made her way to the solar, followed closely by Stuart. There she found Sir William looking out the window with a spyglass.

"Stuart says soldiers are coming. Is that true?" asked Judith.

"I'm afraid so," said Sir William. "I cannot yet tell whose they are, but I would estimate a couple of hundred horse."

"Do you think they're coming here?" asked Judith apprehensively.

"It would appear they are," said Sir William. "They're already starting up the south hill."

"Let me see," demanded Judith, taking the spyglass. She looked and could see a sea of men and horses fast approaching Chapman Hall, but they were still too far away to be identified, as neither side wore actual uniforms.

"May I look, too?" asked Stuart.

He took the spyglass from his mother.

"Mother! It's Father—and Uncle Geoff! I see their standards! I remember them from when we visited the camp at Easter! They're coming home!"

Almost throwing the spyglass at his mother, Stuart bounded down the stairs and out the south door. He ran to the foot of the garden, and by the time Judith and Sir William arrived on the terrace, Richard had already scooped him up onto his horse.

In all the excitement of welcoming home the victorious warriors, Richard and Judith barely had a minute alone with each other. The soldiers, under the direction of Captain Johnson and the captain of Geoff's regiment, set up their tents all around Chapman Hall, and the house staff brought out everything in the house that was edible or drinkable. The family dined with the two captains in the dining room. There was much toasting all around, with questions from Sir William and Stuart about the conduct of the battle. Captain Johnson was full of praise for Richard's soldiering, and both Sir William and Stuart were proud to be related to him.

Finally Richard and Judith and the boys made their way upstairs. Richard kissed Judith tenderly, promising to await her in her bed while she tucked in the boys. She hurried through her bedtime tasks, but when she crawled into bed, Richard was sound asleep.

The regiments were up before dawn as usual and had begun striking their tents when a rider came from the Earl of Newcastle, who had spent the night just up the road at Bolling Hall, home of the Tempest family. The Earl's plan had been to attack Bradford and put to rest completely the region's opposition to the king.

The light of day saw a different plan, however. There would be no attack. Bradford, a wool town with no defenses, would be too easy a target, and innocent people would die. Fairfax's army had already left the area and was headed east. As it turned out, a small part of the royal army, who had not yet received word of the change, did have a skirmish with the citizens of Bradford, in which a dozen armed men were killed, but that was it.

This change in plans was so drastic that even people who saw the logic of it sought some other explanation, and a legend grew (perhaps started by Newcastle himself) that Newcastle had been visited during the night by a ghost, who begged him to "Pity poor Bradford."

Since some of their wounded were still in no condition to ride, the two captains, with the approval of Geoff and Richard, decided to wait a few more days before setting off for Oxford, especially since there was ample space for drilling on Richard's fallow fields. Richard was of two minds about this: on the one hand, it would give him more time with his family and ensure that Parliamentary deserters did not menace them; on the other, it might strain the resources of his flocks and storehouses. Nevertheless, his men deserved a rest, so he tried to be positive.

He spent each morning drilling with the men. Captain Johnson wanted to discuss with the men how they had done in the battle and how they could improve. He had had the chance to observe much before the regiment's entrance into the battle and in its aftermath, and he wanted to impart the new strategies he had learned (some from Fairfax's men). Listening to him, Richard realized just how green he himself still was. He had been such a bundle of nerves going into the battle that he had seen nothing of what the captain had seen.

Each afternoon he rode around the estate with his father and Stuart, verifying that all was as it should be. New lambs abounded in the pastures, and the crops of oats and barley were green and healthy. Sir William rattled on as they rode, obviously delighted to show Richard how capably he had managed. Every now and then, Stuart chimed in, and Richard could see that grandfather and grandson were enjoying their time together and that Stuart was getting a first-class education in farming. It was bittersweet for him to see them doing so well without him.

His evenings were for Benjy and Judith. Benjy wanted to show him the books that the curate, his tutor, had provided him, all books that Richard had read in his own childhood and was happy to read with Benjy. He remembered well his hornbook that had taught him his alphabet and the book of Aesop's fables that had probably had more influence on his moral development than he had realized, as well as the children's Bible that had first acquainted him with the great figures of the Old and New Testaments.

Once the boys had been put to bed, Richard and Judith had time to themselves. After their hungry lovemaking, which both had missed terribly during their time apart, they talked, sharing their experiences. Judith's were full of homely anecdotes about the boys and the house, Richard's of the training camp and its personalities.

At first, he refused to talk about the battle, but finally, one night after a visit to the wounded, he told Judith what it was like in a battle.

"It wasn't as bad as I thought it would be," he admitted to Judith, "and I worry about that. I thought I would freeze up and be unable to fight, but that didn't happen. It was as though my mind no longer controlled my body. I did what I had been trained to do and never thought about the fact that I was wounding and maybe killing other human beings. It makes me feel like some kind of barbarian, not a Christian. How can I call myself one when I'm doing the opposite of what Jesus said—loving my enemies?"

"Did you feel hatred for them?" Judith asked.

"No, I just didn't feel anything, as though I was sleep-walking or something."

"Have you asked Geoff about it?" Judith inquired. "Does he feel the same way?"

"No, I haven't," said Richard. "I'm afraid he'll think I'm a coward."

"Richard, how could he?" said Judith. "We all heard what Captain Johnson said about you, that you're a really fine soldier. You didn't run away; you were there and fought like all the rest!"

"Yes, I did," acknowledged Richard, "but Geoff seems so comfortable with it all, and I'm not in the least comfortable. I dread having to do it again."

"I'm praying that you won't," said Judith. Maybe this victory will cause Parliament to get off its high horse and go along with the king."

"If only that could come to pass!" said Richard. "I would be so glad never to see a bleeding man with a leg cut off or a dead body with its eyes open but seeing nothing. When I try to sleep, it all comes back to me, and I weep for those men and their families and pray that God will forgive me for my part in it!"

"My darling Richard," said Judith, kissing the tears that were starting to run down his cheeks, "as if God would judge you for what those wicked Parliamentarians are forcing you to do!"

Richard kissed her back, but his thoughts were different: for what the king's desire for power has forced me to do. He kept his own counsel, though, knowing that Judith would never understand and in many ways grateful for her innocence of the evils of the world.

Within minutes, she was sound asleep, but sleep was to be a stranger to him for yet another night.

On the fourth day after the battle of Adwalton Moor, Captain Johnson called Richard aside to say that with Richard's permission, they would begin their march toward Oxford the next day. It was not welcome news to Richard, but he agreed. If it had to happen, it might as well do so. The dread and the waiting were driving him mad.

By dawn he was yet again saying goodbye to his family. How many more goodbyes would there be before this bloody mess was over?

The two regiments headed southeast to Oxford. There they were greeted with joy by the king, who was elated by the Adwalton victory, which gave him control of all of Yorkshire except the city of Hull. Both Geoff and Richard received knighthoods, and the two regimental captains were made colonels, contingent on need. That is, if future battles required uniting several cavalry troops under one leader, either of these men had authorization to lead them. The knighthoods that Richard and Geoff received carried little benefit except the respect accorded being called "Sir."

They were unable to rest on their laurels, however, as they received word that Newcastle needed them in Lincolnshire, so they headed that way, helping Newcastle to capture Gainsborough and Lincoln before following him toward Hull, where Fairfax had gone after Adwalton Moor and had fortified his position. This was an important assignment for Geoff, as his family's lands were so close to Hull and their businesses in the port itself, and Richard was happy for Judith's sake that he could assist.

In September of 1643, Newcastle tried to recapture Hull but was unsuccessful, and on October 12 he gave up and retreated to York. To make matters worse, on September 25, the signing of the Solemn League and Covenant had secured a military alliance between the English Parliament and the Scottish Covenanters.

The Royalist army was dispirited by these military and diplomatic setbacks, but Richard was able to go home for a few weeks after this and was able to spend Christmas with his family.

His joy was short-lived, however, when in early January of 1644 his regiment was summoned to assist Col. John Belasyse in patrolling the Royalist holdings in Yorkshire. "This is the price of our success, I suppose," Richard cynically told Judith and his father. "Belasyse is priding himself on his fast-moving horse, and he apparently thinks we fit that description."

As spring approached, the effects of the alliance with the Scots began to be felt, and this development, coupled with heavy snow through England's mid-section, where much of the army was, was demoralizing to the Royalists.

Then in March, the Parliamentarians recaptured Bradford. This time, Richard was happy to participate in Belasyse's attempt to retake the city, so close to his home, but that attempt was also unsuccessful, and in April, Parliament even took Selby, where Belasyse had moved his headquarters. Fortunately, the Royalist cavalry, including Richard, was able to escape, and Richard rushed home, where he was relieved to find that his family and estate, miraculously, it seemed to him, had not been harmed. After a visit that seemed much too short, Richard rejoined his regiment, which was regrouping at York. He had lost a couple of men since Adwalton Moor, but Andrew Selden had replaced them from regiments that had not fared as well as his had. Richard insisted on continuing to pay to the families the wages of the men who had died, though he knew he was just adding to his already huge debt.

The new members of the regiment had barely enough time to learn everyone's name when the battle at Marston Moor brought disaster to the regiment. Parliament beat the Royalists so badly that in two hours the Royalist army lost over 4,000, and 1,500 Royalists were taken prisoner. York surrendered two weeks later. At this point, Parliament controlled Yorkshire. Richard and the remainder of his regiment followed Prince Rupert to Chester to rebuild the Royalist army. Newcastle, finally admitting defeat, fled to the Netherlands.

Rebuilding was not easy. Whereas previously Richard had lost only a couple of men, Marston Moor had cost about a third of the regiment. Again Andrew Selden was able to supply replacements from other horse troops, but these newcomers had not had the benefit of the excellent skills of Captain Johnson, and they had to unlearn bad habits before they could learn good ones. As Richard watched their inept drills, he groaned inwardly at the thought of what they were costing him and what they might cost him in loss of life in future battles.

As a result of this delay and training, the regiment did not see action again until June of 1645, when they faced the combination of Fairfax's forces and the New Model Army under Oliver Cromwell. Prince Rupert's patched-together army was no match, and this battle at Naseby was decisively won by Parliament, with the Royalists losing 1,000 and Parliament only 150.

A number of the losses were from Richard's newly reconstituted regiment: most the newcomers, but some veterans who became the victims of the newcomers' mistakes, including one who had been with him from the beginning, the man called Piers. Richard himself had a few close calls.

It took many months for the regiment to recover from this battle. Again, at great expense, Richard had to hire new members, while still paying the families of the deceased, and the regiment had to go into training.

Having gone home to celebrate Christmas with their families, by the beginning of 1646 the regiment was ready to join they rest of the army. This time they were assigned to assist Sir Jacob Astley in engaging Parliament near Stow-on-the-Wold in the Cotswolds. Astley commanded a force of about 3,000, Parliament a slightly smaller number. The Parliamentary forces were led by Col. Thomas Morgan and Sir William Brereton.

At first, the Royalists did well, but then Brereton's cavalry attacked the Royalist cavalry on the right flank, and the Royalists fled, leaving the king to surrender to Parliament.

Among the Royalist dead was Richard Chapman. As he had tried to rally his fleeing men to stand and fight, one of his new recruits was picked off by a musketeer and knocked Richard as he fell off his horse. Richard tried to recover, but in the melee, his own horse reared, and he was thrown to the ground, breaking his neck. He died instantly.

Geoff, Captain Johnson, and Jeremy had survived the battle of Stow-on-the-Wold without significant injury, but all three felt wounded in spirit at the thought of returning Richard's body to his family. They decided that they owed it to Richard to accompany his body to Yorkshire.

First, Geoff sent a message to his mother, telling her the news and asking her to be the one to go to Chapman Hall and tell Judith. He felt Diana would be able to break the news as gently as possible and would help Judith to deal with it.

Next, he set about getting a box built and finding an embalmer. The journey would not be short, and he knew Judith would want to see Richard's body before his burial. Without embalming, that would be impossible.

Thus, a full week had elapsed by the time the somber procession took the road north, its sad cargo on one of the regiment's supply wagons. Jeremy, who had the most experience in driving a wagon, took on that task, and his horse walked along beside the wagon.

Word of the battle had arrived at Chapman Hall, and Judith was like a caged animal waiting for news from either Richard or Geoff. She knew things had gone badly for the Royalists, and she imagined her beloved husband and cherished brother lying bleeding on the battlefield. She roamed the house for hours on end, up and down stairs, west wing to east wing, unable to settle down.

Stuart and Benji, who had not been told the news about the battle, discussed between themselves what might be wrong with their mother. "I wonder if she's going to have another child, " Stuart said to Benjy. "I don't remember how she acted when you were born. I was too little, but I heard Giles say about his wife that she always acted strangely when she was with child."

"That must be it," agreed Benjy. "Alisande was certainly not herself when she was about to calve. Maybe it's the same with people."

Stuart immediately agreed, and the matter was settled. For a nine-year-old and a seven-year-old boy, females must be all the same, whether the family's favorite milk cow or their mother.

The boys were on the south terrace playing when the sound of coach wheels and horse hoofs called their attention to the road rounding the hill on which the house sat. As the coach got closer, both boys recognized it as that of their Waldby grandparents and the rider who accompanied it as their grandfather. They ran into the house screaming for their mother, who had gone up into the solar and was sitting on the bed holding Richard's favorite lap robe to her chest. Judith hurtled down the stairs when she heard the boys and was with them at the north door when the coach pulled up. Sir Henry scooped first Judith and then the boys into his arms, then opened the coach door and helped Diana to descend. She, too, gave hugs and kisses all around and followed everyone into the house.

The minute she saw her parents' faces, Judith knew something was wrong, but she didn't ask because the boys were there. She shepherded everyone into the parlor and called for refreshments, making small talk awkwardly, trying to ignore the lump that was rising in her throat like some noxious, poisonous apple, choking the life and soul out of her.

Finally, the curate arrived for the boys' afternoon lessons, and she was able to be alone with her parents.

"What has happened?" she asked, standing and speaking as calmly as she could force herself to be. "Why are you here?"

"Oh, Judith!" wailed Diana, rushing to Judith and pulling her into her arms. "It's Richard, Judith, sweet, brave Richard! He didn't make it through that horrible battle. Oh, it's just too much to bear!"

Something delicate and brittle cracked inside Judith, and her knees gave way. Sir Henry caught her in his arms and gently sat her in a chair. "He died a hero, Judith," he stumbled, the only words of consolation he could think of at the moment.

For some minutes Judith just sat as if in a trance. Then her tears began to flow, and great sobs wracked her body. Her parents let her grief spend itself, Diana weeping as well, and Sir Henry blinking back tears of empathy for his daughter's suffering.

Finally, Judith was able to compose herself somewhat. "And Geoff?" she said hoarsely.

"Right as rain," offered Sir Henry. "Barely a scratch. Should be here in a few days, I'll warrant."

"Yes," said Diana. "He'll be bringing Richard back to you, Judith. He wouldn't trust it to anyone else."

"Of course not," said Judith, starting to weep again. "I would have expected nothing less from Geoff. Thank God he's safe, at least." With that, Judith's face once more became trancelike.

Her parents were quiet for some minutes; then Sir Henry said, "Would you like for me to tell the boys?"

"No," said Judith. "Thank you, but I want to tell them myself. I hope you'll be here with me when I do, though. Let's let them have their lesson in peace. There will be plenty of time for grieving. We must send to Richard's parents first, in any case." She summoned Colin and asked him to ride to the elder Chapmans' and ask them to come, on the pretext of having dinner with her parents.

Sophia and Sir William were as devastated as Judith expected them to be. The usually so competent Sophia was reduced to incoherence at the loss of her only child, and Sir William drowned in guilt for his not having listened to Richard's reservations about joining the king. In their blissful bucolic home, they had heard nothing of the battle.

When the boys were finally summoned and told, they, too, reacted as expected. Whereas Benjy gave full vent to his grief with sobs and howls, Stuart, reserved like his father, just stared stony-faced. "It's not true," he said. "It's one of Uncle Geoff's pranks. If father were dead, I would know it, and I don't."

"Oh, Stuart, how we all wish it weren't so, but it is!" cried Judith.

"I won't believe it until I see him," said Stuart stoically. "He'll come riding up the drive the way he has done each time before, and we'll all have a laugh. You'll see."

As there was no changing his mind, the family turned their thoughts to the immediate needs of dinner and the planning of Richard's funeral. Since they did not know which day the body would arrive, they could not set a date, but they could consult the vicar for proper procedures, which they did.

Finally, almost a week after the arrival of the Waldbys, the caravan made its dirge-like way to the doors of Chapman Hall. A bier had been set up in the parlor, and Jeremy and Captain Johnson helped to transfer the body from its crude pine box to the ornate black oak coffin the family had brought in. It was one of two that Sophia had commissioned for herself and Sir William, never dreaming that their child would precede them in death.

After the transfer, Judith and the boys were brought in. Because he had not been wounded and had been embalmed quickly after his death, Richard looked as though he was sleeping. How many mornings had Judith awakened and looked at that handsome face as he slept! Her tears flowed copiously at the thought that she would never see that living face again.

Stuart, ever optimistic, tried to nudge his father awake, and when he was unsuccessful and was finally convinced that his father was dead, broke from his mother and fled to his room, locking the door behind him. No pleas from Judith or remonstrances from his grandfathers and uncle succeeded in getting him to come out, so the family finally left him to handle his grief in his own way. Benjy was inconsolable at first but eventually let the curate lead him away to pray for his father in the parish church.

At dinner that night, Captain Johnson and Jeremy, who were invited to eat with the family, consoled them with stories of Richard's valor and his care for his soldiers. "Those men will not forget him anytime soon," said the captain, "nor will I. I have never met a man who treated his fellow human beings more justly. Lady Chapman, I will give you a list of the surviving men in the regiment. If you ever need anything, all you need to do is send for them, and they'll be here as soon as is humanly possible. I will notify as many as I can once the funeral arrangements are made. I know that if they can, they'll come."

"Thank you, Captain," said Judith. "Your words gladden my heart. Richard was so afraid that other soldiers would think him a coward because he feared and hated fighting. I'm glad that they respected him instead."

"Coward? Sir Richard?" said Jeremy, incredulous. "If he felt that way, he was even braver than I thought. When a person is afraid but fights anyway, that person is a brave man—much braver than I am. When I'm on the battlefield, I feel hate for the enemy and just want to mow him down."

"You don't seem that kind of person to me," said Judith, "but I do know that Richard felt nothing but pity for the men he killed, and he would have undone their deaths if it had been possible."

"I have known Richard for a long time," said the curate, "and I'm sure his goodness sent him straight to Heaven."

"You are so right," added Goeff. "Richard was a truly good man."

Fortunately, the planning of the funeral and the arrivals of friends and family took up all of the family's time and most of their attention, so they were not able to dwell on their loss.

Only Stuart refused to take part in any of the preparations. He spent his days riding his pony through all of the areas he and Richard had ever ridden, and he stopped often, thinking of what his father had done and said on each occasion. The time he had missed with his father because of the war weighed heavily on him, and he decided that if he ever became the soldier he wanted to become, he would not marry and have children. He did not want others to suffer the way he was suffering.

Benji was able to channel his grief into helping the curate with the funeral plans and listening to the curate's stories about his father and telling the curate all he remembered during his brief life, from which Richard had been so much absent because of the war.

Judith went to her room completely spent every night, having held her grief in like an apronful of apples and finally letting it cascade into paroxysms of sobs until her exhausted body finally succumbed to sleep.

Finally all was ready for the funeral. There was no need to hire a "searcher," as the cause of Richard's death was evident. Nor did they need to hire mourners, since Richard was so well liked that people came and honestly mourned his passing. The service in the village church was poignant, with both Geoff and the curate giving eulogies, and Richard was buried with his ancestors in the churchyard. A celebratory feast at Chapman Hall followed, and at last it was all over. Judith almost dreaded that moment, knowing that with nothing to distract her, she would have to come to terms with losing him.

Part IV

Having left Chapman Hall, Captain Johnson and Jeremy parted ways at Halifax, Captain Johnson going southeast to visit his parents in Stratford and Jeremy going farther southeast to Lincolnshire. The captain found his family safe and well, though mourning the loss of three cousins who had perished in the fighting.

Jeremy found his father the same, chiding Jeremy for having left him so much work and expecting him to fall right back into farming life. Jeremy was miserable. On the battlefield, he was somebody. In his village, he was no one. He immediately began looking for a way to escape again.

It was obvious that the royal army was finished. He thought about switching sides, but he had come to hate the puritanical ways of their neighbors who were supporters of Parliament, and he could not imagine fighting alongside people who had been his enemies so recently. Besides, since the king had surrendered to the Scots on May 5, maybe there would be no more fighting. Of course, there was always the Continent. Those people, the captain had told him, were always fighting with each other, so except for brief times of peace, there would always be a fight to join. With that in mind, Jeremy began to save his money for passage across the channel.

As it turned out, his worries were unnecessary. He had not been home a month when Capt. Johnson turned up on his doorstep. The captain was equally bored with life in his hometown and was looking for something else to do. He had made a trip to London and had found out that a man who had emigrated to America in the 1630s had come to England looking for a few experienced men to take to Virginia to help train the local militias. The captain wanted Jeremy to join him. Jeremy was only too glad to do so. He had heard at his mother's knee how wonderful life was in the colonies, where everyone was free, and birth and position didn't matter. He wondered where his mother had come by that information and why it had seemed so important to her, but her enthusiasm had left in him a desire to see those wonderful colonies that had so captured her imagination and therefore his. He happily said farewell to his father and sister and rode away with the captain. On their way to London, they recruited a number of their former colleagues and set sail for Virginia.

At first things went well, but the increasing numbers of English colonists were making the natives nervous. They had begun to realize that these newcomers did not think of property in the way that they did, and that if they did not act, they would be overrun. Moreover, the English had broken several promises to the natives and had even killed some of them, placing their heads on pikes for all to see. Angry about this and egged on by the French and the Dutch, who were making inroads into territory the English considered theirs, a band of natives attacked and set fire to the wooden village/fort where Jeremy and his colleagues were stationed. The English vowed revenge.

The attack on the native village would take place at noon. The scout had informed the captain that in the summer the Potawameck normally took their midday meal at around 11:00. Then they lay about under the trees in retreat from the heat until almost 2:00, after which they resumed their daily tasks. This captain was not Capt. Johnson but a local militiaman whom Capt. Johnson had trained. Jeremy went along as second in command to monitor the new captain's progress. Capt. Johnson remained at the fort training another militia.

The sun was shining brightly as the troop rode off, the heat and humidity causing the soldiers to be drenched with perspiration before they were well out of the fort. Though the king was a captive of Parliament, His Majesty's dragoons must wear their padded leather vests and red woolen sashes, no matter what the temperature in this Virginia hellhole. Jeremy cursed the king and the captains (both Johnson and the one who was with him on the raid) and the natives and the French and the Dutch and himself for having gotten himself into this situation. He must have been crazy to volunteer for this duty. No women except these disgusting savages, poor rations, limited rum, and this damned heat! He'd be better off plowing on his father's farm, damn him.

By the time the troop reached the native village, Jeremy was madder than any hornet. His fingers alternately tapped nervously on his sabre hilt and clicked the trigger of his matchlock musket. He'd kill some savages that day!

They expected the village to be quiet, so they left the horses upstream and walked down the riverside. Their scout had reported that the natives did not post sentinels. Believing themselves protected by their friends the French, they did not expect trouble from any quarter.

Nevertheless, as the English approached the village, they found the silence ominous. Even during the afternoon rest period, surely there would have been some noise, the sound of a baby crying, anything. But there was nothing.

Alarmed, the British advanced warily, each soldier moving from one tree or brush cover to another. Their boots made crackling sounds on the forest floor, and they looked apprehensively at one another, expecting any minute an unpleasant surprise.

None came. They walked into the middle of the village unchallenged. The captain threw back the skins covering the first door of one of the longhouses. The longhouse was empty. Similar checks revealed the same. The village was empty.

"Where are they?" whispered a soldier at Jeremy's left.

"I don't know," replied the captain. "Maybe they're all sleeping in the woods on the north side, where it's cooler. Let's go."

The troop then moved to the north. Their voices by then had disturbed the natives, who were indeed sleeping in the woods. However, there were only women and children.

The captain grabbed one woman who had gathered her three babies around her and was cringing near a tree. "Where are your men?" he demanded.

The woman, who did not understand English, merely stared at

him, eyes big with fear.

"Where are your men?" the scout repeated in the Algonquian language. The woman said something and pointed north. "She says they went to hunt early this morning. They'll be back at nightfall. She says the women will host us until their husbands return. Then we can talk to them."

"Well," said the captain, "we can't refuse an invitation like that, can we?" The woman who had spoken was young, probably no more than twenty, and quite attractive for a native. The captain grabbed her by the wrist and pulled her toward him with one hand, throwing the children aside with the other. She shrieked, and other women rushed to help her, only to be grabbed themselves by soldiers. "Let's teach these savage bastards what it means to attack Englishmen!" the captain shouted, forcing the woman to the ground.

A chorus of "Long live the king!" almost drowned out the screams of the terrified women.

Jeremy spied his as she broke for the village. She was slender and large-bosomed, and her breasts bounced under her deerskin shift as she ran. Anger and lust rose in him together, and he ran after her, catching up with her as she tried to enter one of the longhouses through a door facing the river. He spun her around and threw her to the ground on her back, knocking her unconscious on the slender log that formed the threshold of the longhouse door. As her body went limp, he pulled up her shift and, tearing the buttons from his uniform trousers, thrust into her, his hands grabbing for her breasts and holding them like reins.

As he spurted his seed inside the woman, he let out a triumphant yell and did not hear the movement behind him as a native raised his tomahawk and brought it down with deadly force on Jeremy's head. His skull was cloven in two so completely that the edge of the blade nicked the native woman's chin. His blood mingled with hers as the man, her husband, yanked Jeremy's body off hers and hacked at his member with his tomahawk until it was nothing but a bloody mess.

The rest of the troop met a similar fate. A few were able to put up a fight, but no native men received more than superficial wounds, and all the British were killed except the scout, whose occupation had made him a little more circumspect about such things. He had not taken part in the mass rape but rather, at the time the natives arrived, was searching the area to the north, the direction from which, according to what the woman had said, they could expect the men to return. When he became aware of what was taking place and realized that the woman had lied, he continued north as quickly as possible. By the time the men finished wreaking vengeance on the British, he was far away and returned to the fort by another route.

His news left the remaining British utterly demoralized. The heat, their small numbers, especially with the loss of a whole troop, and the fact that the natives, who had formerly felt secure, would now be on the lookout for an attack force, more than balanced their anger that their fellow soldiers had been hacked to pieces by the natives, especially because of the actions of the British that had precipitated that defeat. There was still some humanity left, even on the frontier.

Accordingly, the commandant of the fort decided to withdraw as soon as possible to the coast. The natives could have the territory if they wanted it. It wasn't worth any more English lives, at least not now. If the foreign office decided later to send enough troops to be really effective, then maybe—but not now.

Thus the English departed from the fort. The natives, in their turn, burned the bodies of the dead Englishmen, but not until they had mutilated every one of them. A normally peaceful tribe, they had not been the ones who had burned the fort, and they had cooperated with the English more out of genuine friendliness and a desire for trade than anything else, but now they became mistrustful of all Europeans, continuing to deal with the English on only a limited basis, usually only with an occasional traveling merchant who came to the village alone, with only a pack mule to haul the goods of his commerce.

The women of the village put themselves through a purification ritual to cleanse themselves of the filth of their rapists, but none of the kwiocosuk's ministrations could erase the nightmares that awakened them at night when they accidentally touched their husbands' bodies in their sleep or could calm the midnight screams of the children who had witnessed the violations of their mothers, sisters, aunts, and even grandmothers. That horrible day lay long in the tribe's memory, along with the time of famine that had preceded it by many moons and the war with the Iroquois that had happened so long before that not even the oldest woman in the village remembered anyone who had been an eyewitness.

Only one pregnancy resulted from the rape. Sun Woman, wife of a prominent leader of the village, remained unconscious for many hours after Jeremy raped her. Her husband, who loved her dearly, was so afraid for her life that he would not let anyone touch her. Thus she missed out on the cleansing which the other women happily embraced and was unable to swallow the bitter liquid that would have caused her to abort a fertilized egg. When it became obvious that she was pregnant, no one knew, of course, whose the child was; it was only after the baby was born, a little girl with blue eyes and curly black hair, that her parentage became obvious. Sun Woman, like any good mother, loved her daughter, no matter who her father was; besides, she had been blissfully unaware of the rape, since she was unconscious the whole time and since the blow to her head and the concussion it had caused had removed all memory of it from her mind. Her husband, a reasonable man, did not blame the child for her origins and felt he had removed all taint from his wife by himself killing her attacker.

Part V

After Richard's funeral, Judith forced herself to concentrate on the needs of her sons. She accompanied Stuart on his rides, often getting Benjy to come along, letting the boys tell her everything Richard had said at each place. They all took comfort in remembering happier times with him. On the way home each time, Judith made sure to steer them to the tree under which Richard had first kissed her, the time when she thought she had lost him by being too free with her favors. What a long-ago, oh-so-innocent time that seemed!

When the boys were busy with their lessons with the curate, she roamed the house, visiting all the rooms aimlessly, cudgeling her brain to remember every single thing Richard had said or done in every single room. She remembered all their plans for finishing the decorating of the house after the war, which they both thought would be brief. What was the point now, without him?

One of her favorite places was the solar, where he had slept during her postpartum confinements and when the boys were little and likely to awaken during the night in the cradle that sat right beside her bed and later in the trundle that pulled out from beneath it. It would not have been logical to deprive the master of the house of his rest when he had so much to do all day long. How had they managed during his absences? Judith wondered. Giles and Sir William had been wonderful, keeping the estate in good order and running beautifully while Richard was away for weeks at a time during the war, though she hadn't seen too much of Sir William since the funeral. She supposed he and Sophia needed time to deal with their grief by themselves.

The solar was an almost bare room high in the old tower. In it, Richard slept on a plain wooden bedstead that had belonged to generations of Chapmans before him. Unlike the more decorated rooms of the house, the walls were not covered with wooden panels. Rather, the centuries-old stone was hung with stiff linen canvas, painted with the Chapman coat of arms. The small fireplace was lined with simple, uneven stones, but the chimney drew well, and even on chilly days, Judith felt its warmth, though it lacked the radiant glow of Richard's presence.

The other place that attracted her was Richard's study on the ground floor, where he had kept the estate's accounts. For the first few weeks, she contented herself with just sitting on the settee, sensing his presence, smelling his fragrance, and weeping. She gained some solace from handling his belongings: his globe, his telescope with which he delighted the boys by showing them the moon and the planets. Geoff had put Richard's armor in the study when he brought Richard's body home, but Judith had removed them to the solar, which she saw as more appropriate.

After some time, when her grief had somewhat spent itself, she began to look through the papers in his lift-top desk. Among them, she found his contract with Andrew Selden, along with the additions Richard had made regarding paying the families of his men who had been killed or badly injured. She wept again at his loyalty to the king, remembering how little he trusted Charles, and at his generosity.

When she saw the solicitor's name on the papers, she thought about contacting him to make sure all was well but then thought better of it, knowing she had no knowledge of such things and would not be helpful. She preferred to wait until she could speak to Sir William about it.

Sir William, however, was as ignorant of what Richard had done as she was. He was appalled when he read the papers and realized that Richard had mortgaged the entire Chapman estate.

"What was he thinking?" protested Sir William. "He must have taken leave of his senses! No one wagers all that he possesses. That Selden fellow would have been happy with a fraction of the value of this property!"

"But Sir William," said Judith, "it seems that Richard has already paid him a great deal yet till owes much more. I had no idea that we made so much money each year! Do you think we'll be able to continue making the payments every year until the debt is paid off?"

"We may if we stop all this foolishness about paying the families of the dead soldiers," said Sir William. "No one does that! It's folly! We'll go broke! Only thirty soldiers survived that last battle. We can't support seventy more families!"

"But it's what Richard wanted to do," pleaded Judith.

"Judith, my ancestors and I have slaved over this land for centuries," said Sir William. "I will not have it lost because Richard was ridiculously generous. It belongs to Stuart and Benjy now. They deserve for us to keep it for them."

Judith had to see his point. Although she hated not to do what Richard had wanted, she realized how difficult it would be to support that many people.

"What about giving their wives and sons jobs on the estate if they need them? Could we do that?" she asked.

"Well," said Sir William, "if they come around and need work, and we need help, we can certainly give them preference."

That satisfied Judith, and she wrote a letter to the solicitor telling him her decision. She did not realize from how far afield the men in the regiment had come until she found and read the list of surviving soldiers that Captain Johnson had given her. Her heart sank when she had to admit to herself that it was unlikely that any of the families of the dead or wounded soldiers would ever show up on her doorstep.

For the first two years after Richard's death, with most of the conflict occurring in the south, the Chapman estate prospered. The demand for wool and barley remained steady, the weather cooperated, and trade with the Continent resumed after its wartime disruptions. Sir William made frequent trips to Hull to negotiate with Judith's uncle regarding wool shipments and always returned optimistic.

Meanwhile, Geoff had returned to Waldby House with his parents and siblings. With his regiment ruined, it would be months, if not years, given the disarray of the country, before he could mount a fighting force again, and Richard's death had left him sick of warfare. He would let the more powerful of the land squabble over politics now that the king was in custody. (Ironically, the king's Scottish countrymen, whose protection he had sought, had handed him over to Parliament just months after his surrender to them.) Instead, Geoff set his sights on finding a wife and settling down. He doubted that he would be happy on the estate but thought he might join his uncle in the wool business in Hull. Second son or no, Stephen could have the estate.

For his part, Stephen was feeling left out. He had reached the age of majority and was ready to take his place in defense of his king. By the time the family had reached Waldby House after Richard's funeral, Stephen had shared his plans to outfit a regiment of his own. Geoff tried as hard as he could to dissuade him, especially as the news was that the war had devolved into mostly local squabbles, most in the London area, far away from Yorkshire, but he was not successful. Even worse, Stephen had talked Sally's husband, Alex, into joining him. It would cost less for each, they said, if they paid for the regiment together.

"Stephen," Geoff exploded, "you and Alex are idiots! Neither of you knows the first thing about fighting. You'll be killed! This new army under Oliver Cromwell is a pack of demons. They'll slice you to bits."

"Well, Richard didn't know about fighting either," argued Stephen, "and look how well he did."

"Yes, and look how dead he is now," replied Geoff.

"I think he got killed only because he was afraid," insisted Stephen. "Everyone admits that he hated fighting. I don't. I look forward to skewering some Roundheads. I'll get even for Richard."

"Stephen, Richard wouldn't want revenge. He wasn't that kind of man. Richard hated fighting because he saw how stupid and useless it was. I wish I had known him sooner. I wouldn't have wasted my time learning soldiering. I used to think war was glorious. It's not. Besides, Richard was one of the bravest men I've ever known. Everyone agreed on that. You heard those men from his regiment."

"Well, of course they'd say that at his funeral," said Stephen.

"What would you expect them to say, that their leader was a coward? Face it, Geoff, Richard was a handsome man and a nice person, but he was no soldier. I could see it in his eyes."

"Stephen, I only pray that this mess gets settled soon and you don't ever have to go into battle. You won't last a day," said Geoff sorrowfully. "I don't want to lose my little brother."

"Don't worry, Geoff. I'll make you proud. You'll see," said Stephen.

Alex proved to be just as stubborn. By the time Geoff got to him, he had already engaged Andrew Selden to procure what he and Stephen needed.

"Alex, how could you?" demanded Geoff. "It's bad enough for Stephen, who is single, but you have a wife and children. Didn't you see the state Judith and the boys were in? Do you want that for Sally and your daughters?"

"Of course not," replied Alex, "but…."

Geoff cut him off. "But nothing. What do you think will happen to Judith now? She may be all right for a few years, as long as Sir William is alive to handle things, but then will she have to marry some slimy Puritan just to survive? It will be years before her boys are old enough to provide for her. And you have daughters. What will become of them if you're killed or maimed? Think, man, think!"

Nevertheless, Alex was adamant. He saw reason in what Geoff was saying, but he had given his word and had signed the papers. All he could hope was that all would be settled before the regiment was ready to field.

The plans of Stephen and Alex were the deathblow to Geoff's plans. Instead of moving to Hull and finding a city girl to marry, he would be forced to replace Stephen on his father's estate, which was too large for his father to handle alone, and to help Alex's father manage their nearby estate. As Stephen and Alex set off to train in the south, Geoff grumblingly settled into his childhood home.

To ease her worries about Alex, Sally set about (unasked) helping Geoff to find a bride. She did not feel right about organizing parties with Richard so recently buried, but home visits were acceptable, so every time Geoff went to check on the Taylor farms, a young lady or two would just happen to be visiting, and Sally persuaded Diana to do the same with the young ladies in the vicinity of Waldby House.

Finally, after a six-month courtship, Geoff married Catherine Hardgrave, the daughter of a sheep-farming gentleman. The year of mourning for Richard having come to an end, the family was ready to celebrate, and Judith and the boys went to attend the festivities.

As usual when she was unhappy, Judith had lost a great deal of weight, but Clara was able to alter and update one of her old party dresses for the occasion. Being with the Waldby family was wonderful for her and her boys, especially since Stephen and Alex, who had yet to see combat aside from a bit of riot control near London, were able to be there with them. Remembering her own wedding brought both happiness and tears, but she was so happy for Geoff. Catherine was a delightful young woman, and she could see why Geoff had fallen in love with her. She was a beauty indeed, but she was already twenty-six (since few were marrying during the war years), and her relative maturity for the time gave her a sensibleness that Judith admired. She would make Geoff, who, it was clear, had also matured because of the war, a good wife.

Because it was a time of celebration, Judith forbore telling Stephen and Alex what she really thought of their choice, except to tell then how glad she was to see them and how hard she prayed daily for their safety. Stuart and Benjy, of course, greatly enjoyed their army camp stories, as they had those of Richard.

"Master Stuart, your mother would like to speak with you downstairs."

Colin's words startled Stuart, absorbed as he was in his game of chess. What?" he replied, turning towards the door where Colin stood respectfully waiting. "Were you speaking to me, Colin?"

"Yes, Master Stuart, I was. Your mother would like to see you and Master Benjamin downstairs. I am on my way to call Master

Benjamin."

"Very well, Colin. I'll be right down." Stuart carefully put away the chess set. It would not do for anyone to see the moves he was practicing. He picked up the carved ebony pieces, admiring each as he replaced it in its box. Stuart never hurried. For him every moment was precious, and he savored every pleasant experience. His family had grown accustomed to this trait of his and had ceased trying to rush him.

As he was putting the last pawn into the box, Colin again appeared in the doorway. "Master Stuart," he said quietly.

"Yes, Colin?"

"Your mother, Master Stuart."

"Oh! Yes! I had forgotten. Here I come." He slipped on his house shoes, which he had left on the hearth, and followed Colin through the door.

When he reached the bottom of the stairs, he looked around for his mother. She was seated in front of the fireplace in the parlor. Benjy was already seated at her feet on a cushion. Stuart thought his mother looked very serious. In his experience, she looked that way only when something was terribly wrong, such as when she called him in to tell him that his father had been killed in the war. Benjy had been only seven at the time, so Stuart had come alone to be told that his beloved father, the gentle, loving, loyal Richard Chapman, had perished at the battle of Stow-on-the-Wold. Stuart's young heart raced and the blood drained from his face at the thought that some similar catastrophe might have occurred. He was shaking as he pulled a small chair near his mother.

Judith folded her hands in her lap and cleared her throat. Stuart could see that her fingers were rigid, gripping tightly the lacy, embroidered handkerchief she held. "Stuart," she began. "Benjamin. I have something very important to tell you." The tears began to roll down her face. She dabbed her eyes with her handkerchief and took a deep breath, trying to regain her composure. "As you know," she continued, "things have not gone very well for us since your father died. Not only do we all miss him very much, but it has been very hard to take care of our property. Grandfather Chapman and Giles have done a wonderful job, as you know, but Grandfather is getting older and has not been himself since your father died. Grandfather Waldby and Uncle Geoff and Uncle Stephen are themselves busy trying to hold on to what they have left, and Aunt Sally's husband has now also been killed in the war."

"No!" screamed Benjy. "Not Uncle Alex! He can't be dead! Mother, say it's not true!" He pulled at his mother's full skirt and looked pleadingly into her face.

"Oh, Benjy, I should have told you and Stuart before! I'm so sorry. I got word from Aunt Sally last week, but I just couldn't bring myself to tell you. I know how much he meant to you."

"Mother," Benjamin sobbed, burying his face in the folds of her skirt, "Uncle Alex was my friend. I don't even remember my father very well, the way Stuart does. Uncle Alex was like my father. How can he be dead?"

Judith stroked her son's hair, now moist with her own tears. "Oh, Benjy, I don't know. I don't understand anything in this war. I just know it takes everyone you love away!"

Stuart was standing immobile while all of this was going on. The news of his uncle's death brought back all the anguish of that day almost three years before when he had been informed of his father's death. Since that time, life had meant nothing and yet everything to him. His father's death, on the one hand, had left him older than his years, making him only too aware of the transience of life and of the need to make each minute last. But it had also left him closed, unable to express the emotion he felt. He was happiest when he did not have to deal with relationships—they were too painful. Chess and his other games and intellectual and physical pursuits were much easier to deal with. They were his escape. So completely had he withdrawn into them that he thought he had become impervious to emotion, but now this news of his uncle's death and his seeing his brother's grief had brought it all back, and he did not know how to deal with it.

The three of them sat in silence for some minutes, Benjy still sobbing quietly into his mother's skirt and Judith just staring off into space. It was Stuart who spoke first. "Mother, was Uncle Alex's death what you wanted to tell us about?" he asked, knowing full well that that wasn't it at all. If the news about Uncle Alex were the main point, she would not have purposely blurted it out the way she had. Her obvious agitation meant something was really horribly wrong.

Rousing herself from her reverie, Judith looked at Stuart fearfully and lifted Benjy's head with her hands. She took a deep breath. "No, Stuart," she said, "that's not it."

"Then what?" wailed Benjy. "Who else has died without anyone telling me?"

"No one, darling! No one at all," wept Judith. "There's been enough death in this family—more than enough. Boys, it's the estate. We're going to lose it. Your father borrowed money on it to pay for his soldiers, and now the man from whom he borrowed wants his money, and I don't have it!"

"But this is our home, Mother!" screamed Benjy, jumping to his feet. "No one can take it from us!"

"He's right, isn't he, Mother," said Stuart. "This estate has been in our family since the days of the first King William, and Father was a knight. How can someone take it away from us?"

"Being a knight means nothing anymore, Stuart. The Roundheads are in power now. You both know what they did to the king, God rest his soul!" Hot tears streamed down Judith's face. "Why should our titles count for anything? All that matters now is money. Your father borrowed it and signed his name to the contract, and now I don't have it to repay."

"But why, Mother?" asked Benjy, cocking his head to the side and wrinkling his brow. "Didn't we make a good crop this year? Everyone seemed so cheerful."

"Oh, yes, Benjy, we made a beautiful crop, the most beautiful crop we've seen in years," Judith replied. "That's just the problem. Everyone made a good crop, much more than any of us can eat here in England. And what's more, the French made a good crop too, and apparently everyone in Europe, so we can't sell them any of ours. There's so much of everything that everyone has had to lower prices, and no one is making any money!"

"Can't we sell some to the colonies? They have to eat, too," said Benjy hopefully.

"I'm afraid not," said Judith. "There's so much land in the colonies that there's always someone there who has a good crop. They don't need to buy ours. Besides, there aren't enough people there to eat or wear all that we have extra."

"Let me see if I understand this," Stuart said. "We had lots to sell, but we couldn't sell it for the prices we wanted because no one had to buy it from us. So we sold it for what we could get, what people were willing to pay, and what we got wasn't enough to pay what Father borrowed."

"Unfortunately, that's exactly it," said Judith, her shoulders slumping over. "The money lender is coming over here today. I expect that he'll tell us we have to move out and give him the house and the land, since that's what your father mortgaged."

"But where will we go?" said Benjamin. "What will we do?"

"What I wonder is how we will live," said Stuart. "If we have no property, how will we get money to live on?"

"I don't know, boys," said Judith. "I don't know. I hope God knows, because I don't."

"Mother, we have to have some kind of a plan!" entreated Stuart. "We can't just wait for this man to come and kick us out of our own house."

"Yes!" said Benjamin. "Maybe while he's talking to you, Stuart and I can sneak up behind him and shoot him or stab him to death! Then he won't be able to take our home!"

"Benjy! Shame on you!" said Judith. "How can you suggest such a thing?"

"Don't worry, Mother," said Stuart. "He has just been reading too many of the curate's romances. The knights in those things solve all their problems by killing somebody."

"Dear God, I think this family has had enough of killing!" said Judith. "I don't like to hear about it at all, especially from one of my own sons. Benjy, don't you ever talk like that again."

"Mother, scolding Benjy can wait. We have a serious problem here. What can we do? Can we move in with Grandmother and Grandfather Chapman? Can Grandmother and Grandfather Waldby take care of us?"

"Well, I know both sets of grandparents would certainly try, Stuart, and we will certainly go to them first. But I suspect that eventually, the way things are these days, I'll have to marry somebody with money in order for us to survive. My Waldby relatives supported the king too, you know, and they may be heading for worse trouble than we're in. They haven't shared their problems with me."

Benjy, who had slipped into a daydream of knightly attacks while his mother and brother were talking, snapped to attention when his mother said the word "marry."

"Mother!" he said. "You don't mean you'd actually marry someone else? Didn't you love Father?"

Judith began to weep again. "Of course I loved your father, Benjy. I adored your father. But I'm a woman. What can I do? My solicitor says that women can't take care of themselves; they don't have the legal rights. They have to have men to do that!"

"Well," said Benjy, brightening. "Maybe Stuart and I can take care of you."

"Benjy, don't be foolish," said Stuart. "You're ten years old. I'm twelve. What could we do to earn money? We don't even know how to do anything. Why, Giles's grandsons are more capable than we are. They could probably take care of their mother! I used to think it was a good thing to be part of the gentry, but now it seems to be the worst thing in the world! We've let other people do things for us for so long, we can't do anything for ourselves. No wonder the

Roundheads won the war!"

"Stuart!" Judith exclaimed. "How dare you disparage your own family and all of our friends. It was God's will that we should rule over others and they should serve us. Ask any priest; he'll tell you."

"Then he should have told it to the Roundheads," said Stuart. "They didn't seem to have heard. They seem to think God had other ideas."

As he said that, Stuart suddenly felt a chill go up his spine, and he fell silent. He couldn't believe he was hearing his own voice. It was the most he had said at one time since his father's death, and he was expressing an anger he never knew he had inside.

He saw that his mother and brother were as surprised as he was. Both were staring at him open-mouthed. Seeing their faces, he reddened and ran from the room and out of the house and didn't stop running until his exhausted body gave out and he fell into a mindless slumber under a tree in the middle of the game park.

Andrew Selden arrived at Chapman Hall at two o'clock that afternoon. The servant, who he would later find out was named Colin, ushered him into the housebody, the most important room of the house. It was not unlike the one in his father's house, large and bright, with almost the whole of one wall made up of panels of stained glass, with the coats of arms of twenty-four families whose names had been associated with the Chapmans at some point. Although Andrew did not see the Selden crest represented, he did recognize the quartered shield of his mother's family, the Beauforts, and wondered what the connection was.

A woman was seated at the far end of the massive oak table that dominated the room. Her head was down, but she looked up as she heard footfalls on the stone floor and rose to greet Andrew. She wore a black dress and a veil, in mourning for her brother-in-law's death, he assumed, and her face was sorrowful, but Andrew thought she was the most beautiful woman had ever seen, except for Lucy. Dark hair, parted down the middle, was visible under the cap that held her veil, and her eyes were a soft brown. The blackness of her attire made her white skin look even whiter and accentuated her thinness.

As he approached, she held out her gloved hand. "Mr. Selden? I'm Judith Waldby, Lady Chapman."

Andrew took her hand in his, and bowed and kissed it. "Good afternoon, Lady Chapman," he said. "Please accept my condolences on the loss of your husband and, I have just heard, that of your brother-in-law."

"Thank you," Judith said, withdrawing her hand. As Andrew resumed a standing position, he could see that her face was even whiter than when he entered and wondered what he had done to upset her. Perhaps she was surprised at his courtly behavior, having no way of knowing his background. Most of the Royalists whose families he dealt with just assumed he was one of the Puritans they hated. And truthfully, when it came to money, blood meant nothing to him. He hadn't gotten where he was by caring about who was related to whom.

They sat down. Andrew laid the sheaf of papers he was carrying open on the table, and Judith was able to observe him as he laid them out. He was somewhat shorter than Richard, she guessed, but extremely well dressed for a commoner. His hair was neither long nor short but well groomed. He had a small mouth and a nose that seemed too large for the rest of his thin face. He looked a bit like a ferret, Judith thought, but his green eyes were not unkind.

"Now, let's see, Lady Chapman," he said. Your husband, Sir Richard, mortgaged this estate to me in order to purchase what he needed to outfit his troop for battle. This year's payment on that mortgage is now due. How may I expect payment?"

"Mr. Selden, I appreciate your attempt at pleasantry, but you know good and well that I cannot pay you what I owe you. You have been in contact for months with my solicitor in London."

"That is true, Lady Chapman," said Andrew, adjusting himself on the hard, flat wood of his chair, "but I have found that in desperate straits, people sometimes find resources that they never knew they had. This has certainly been true in my life. Moreover, one's solicitor doesn't know everything."

"Well, be that as it may, I don't have the money, and I cannot think of any way that I might get it," said Judith. "I know that in other cases, the estate was lost, and the family had to move out. I have prepared myself and my sons for that eventuality."

"And where will you go, Lady Chapman?" said Andrew, appearing to be genuinely interested. "It's a cruel world out there for a woman and children."

"We will go to my parents, of course, Sir Henry and Lady Waldby."

"Ah, yes, I know your father well," said Andrew. "One of my more affluent clients. However, you may want to reconsider. I happen to know that your father is in debt as well."

He saw her face fall. She really was in a bad situation. Well, that's life, he thought. However, she was very beautiful.

"Lady Chapman," he said, "I know you may have heard that I and my kind are heartless money-grubbers, but I would find it very hard to turn a noble lady like yourself out into the streets, especially with children. Let me propose that you take more time to try to find means to pay these debts. I'm sure that you will be travelling to your family's home to attend your brother-in-law's funeral. Do what you can, and I'll visit you when you return. At that time, you can tell me what progress you've made, and I'll try to advise you on a wise course of action. I seem to have some success where the management of money is concerned."

"You're very kind, Mr. Selden," said Judith with tears in her eyes. "I know that I should just face the truth, that there really is no way out for me, especially now that Father is in trouble as well, but I do want to stay here as long as I can. I have been so happy here, and this house holds so many memories of my dear husband and the births of my children...." Her voice cracked and she could speak no more. She put her face in her hands and sobbed.

Andrew could not see her distress unmoved. He rose and lifted her by her elbows and put his arms around her. His heart went out to this woman in a way he would have never thought possible, and his body responded to her as it had never done since his days with Lucy. "Lady Chapman," he said. "Please don't cry. You won't have to leave this house. We'll work something out."

He felt her relax as her shaking abated, but then her body stiffened and she pulled away from him. "I thank you for your comfort, sir," she said, her voice icy, "as inappropriate as it was for you to offer it to me. I shall gratefully accept your financial advice, but I must ask that you keep a professional distance in the future. It is only money that I owe you!"

"Lady Chapman, I did not mean to offend you," said Andrew, feeling anger rising in him at her condescending rebuff. "Since I have given you my word, I will keep it, but I will not be treated as anything but your equal, which I am in every way. And I assure you, I will keep my distance from you in the future." With that he turned and strode out, not waiting for Colin to show him the door.

Judith's solicitor came from London the next day to see what had transpired with Andrew. When Judith told him what Andrew had told her, and what he had done, the solicitor smiled a knowing smile and said, "Yes, Lady Chapman, that is what I had hoped would happen. Your beauty would turn any man's head, even Andrew Selden's. In fact, especially Andrew Selden's, I had guessed, and it seems that I was right."

"You mean…"

"Yes, Lady Chapman," the solicitor said. "That's why I wanted him to meet you in person. Financially, you haven't a leg to stand on, but a pretty face is very powerful capital."

"Mr. Harris, how dare you suggest that I would sell myself to save my sons' property!" said Judith, her cheeks flushing and anger burning in her eyes.

"Of course not, Lady Chapman. It was indeed crude of me to put it in such terms. But the fact is, Andrew Selden is one of the most eligible bachelors in England. He's rich, he's noble,...."

"Noble! That man?" Judith was astonished.

"Yes, noble, though he wouldn't admit it if you asked him. He renounced his title years ago—some quarrel with his father, I think, but he never did it legally, so technically he is still his father's heir and will one day be Andrew, Lord Selden, Tenth Earl of Wilmot. Whether that will mean anything or not depends on his father's political and financial state. I'm afraid my research into his background didn't go quite that far!"

"Your research?"

"Yes, Lady Chapman," replied the solicitor. "I am a commoner myself, but many of my clients are of the nobility, and this man has been wreaking havoc with their fortunes. He's the cleverest businessman I've ever run across. I've been trying to find the chink in his armor for some time now."

"And?"

"And I've found out that nothing is sacred to him but money. Apparently, his father put the quietus to a youthful romance of his, and he's been a changed man ever since. Never got over the girl or the father's action. Determined to take revenge on the world for what happened. Hates the nobility because his father is noble, and hates the rest of us because his father was aided by one of his servants. He really did that guy in, by the way. Before the war ever started, he got a group of drunken infantrymen who were quartered in the area to set upon this fellow—Oliver Boyle was his name, I think—and tear him limb from limb. Told them he was a French spy—looked a bit French, dark and all, they say, not much difference between the French and the black Irish, same rotten stock."

"And this is the man who holds the title to my estate?" Judith was incredulous. "This is the man to whom you suggest I sell myself?"

"I wish you wouldn't use that word, Lady Chapman," said the solicitor, wincing. "What I'm talking about is marriage, not something vulgar. You are a gentlewoman; he is a nobleman. You would make a perfect match. Since he is going to own your property anyway, why not become his wife and keep it? You'd be secure for life; he's one of the richest men in England."

"How can that be?" Judith said. "You know there's no such thing as security for the nobility anymore."

"Ah, but that's only if they are known supporters of the king," said the solicitor. "And Andrew Selden is not. He cleverly straddled the fence during the war, selling to both sides equally. Besides, there are few who know his noble background. He is a proper chameleon. He affects the clothing and mannerisms of the Puritans when he is with them, and those of the nobility when it suits him. Why, he could disappear into the crowd in Cromwell's chamber and in the French king's court with equal success. What's more, he has lapped up so many estates already by foreclosing on the debts of improvident Cavaliers that no one in Cromwell's government would be surprised if he started putting on the airs of a country gentleman. Indeed, one of his best friends these days is Cromwell's Latin Secretary, a man named John Milton, whose father made his fortune doing just what Selden has done. No, don't you worry; Selden's fortune is secure."

"Nevertheless," said Judith, pulling herself up very straight in her chair, "I could never marry a man I didn't love, and I could never love someone who cared only for money. In fact," and here her shoulders slumped and her voice lost all its proud energy, "I will never love anyone but Richard. How could I? He was the most wonderful man in the world and the father of my children!"

The solicitor, knowing his place better than Andrew had, did not offer to comfort Judith, at least not physically. "Lady Chapman," he said, "no one expects you to love someone else right now. You're still mourning for your husband, and that's as it should be. But you have to be practical. This man is giving you time. He said he would help you to work something out. Let him try. That's the most generous thing I've ever heard of him saying to anyone. If he can fall in love with you, that may change the kind of person he's been. You may become his salvation as he may be yours."

The cessation of Judith's sobbing told the solicitor that his words had had an effect. What woman can resist the opportunity to change a man for the better?

"Do you think that's really possible?" she asked, her blood-shot eyes hopeful.

"I don't see why not," said the solicitor. "If he became the way he is because love was taken from him, why should he not change once he finds love again? He's only forty years old. He would have a miserable life indeed if he continued to lead it all alone. And so, I suspect, would you, Lady Chapman. My grandmother always said that the only women who remain widows are those who hated their husbands and cannot bear the thought of having men in their lives again. If you loved your husband, that's all the more reason you should seek to marry again."

"You seem to be a very wise man, Mr. Harris," said Judith. "Do all solicitors seek to manage their clients' lives and loves as you do?"

"Ah, now that I don't know, Lady Chapman," said the solicitor, smiling. "What I do know is that to be a successful solicitor, one has to understand people and give them the advice they truly need, and one's finances cannot be separated from the rest of one's life, no matter how hard one tries."

"Alas," said Judith, "how I wish that were not so true!"

So it was decided. When Judith and the boys returned from Alex's funeral, Judith would allow Andrew to visit her once a week, and they would look over all her financial records. She was to send to her father for whatever other documents he had that pertained to her situation, and Andrew would look them over as well and see what could be done about her situation. She refused to involve Sophia and Sir William. They had lost so much already. She wondered if the solicitor had let Andrew in on his marriage plot. She doubted it. Surely a man of Andrew's power and reputed hardness would balk at the idea that someone was trying to manipulate his feelings. Moreover, the solicitor had sworn her to secrecy about what he had discovered about Andrew's background. Since the man chose to keep his family a secret, he said, he would not want to be the one through whom the truth got abroad. No "conversion" had yet taken place in Andrew, and the solicitor knew from the experience of some of his colleagues that Andrew had the power to crush anyone he considered his enemy.

She herself didn't believe for a minute that she and Andrew would ever make a match of it, and she had no intention of trying even to like him. It was enough that she would have the opportunity to delay the inevitable. The older the boys got, the sooner they'd be able to take charge, and maybe the next year they'd make more on the crop. Deep inside she knew her hopes were futile, but they were all she had. At least she could keep from antagonizing this man who had such power over her.

At first their visits were quite formal. No matter what her emotional state was that day, Andrew kept his distance, and she did her best to avoid saying anything that could anger him. Actually, knowing that he was of noble blood did change things for her. She no longer looked at him as she had the first time and as she still looked at the solicitor, as a tradesman plying his trade and therefore no more worthy of consideration than the cobbler or the bailiff. Not that she did not see these people as fellow human beings. All who served Judith loved her for her kindness and lack of snobbery, but she had never looked on these people as men.

Andrew, however, was different. He was noble and, being only eight years her senior, might have been one of her suitors if they had known each other as children. In fact, when she inquired of her father as to his knowledge of the Seldens, without saying why she wanted to know, he wrote back that Lord Selden was a person who had been held in great esteem in the House of Lords and who had had the sympathy of everyone when his son disappeared. "Promising lad," her father had written. "I remember meeting him once in London. Had all the marks of success upon him. Pity." She got the impression that word had gotten out that Andrew had been killed somewhere, maybe by savages in the colonies, an increasingly common fate of noble and commoner alike.

In their conversations, she detected nothing of the shrewdness, the sinister calculation that she assumed a man like him would have, but upon remarking on this to the solicitor, she was told, "Of course not, Lady Chapman. And therein lies his real cleverness. When people seem calculating, people put up their defenses. Mr. Selden knows only too well that flies will swarm to honey but avoid vinegar."

And am I to be his next fly? wondered Judith. Then she reminded herself that she was already completely in his power. He had nothing to gain by being nice to her. He already, in effect, owned her property. If he had wanted her person, he could have taken that too. She would not have been the first noblewoman raped under the new regime. She had heard that the real, believing Puritans in Cromwell's army did not transgress the bounds of modesty in their dealings with the women of the defeated nobility. Not everyone in the army was a believing Puritan, however. Some were opportunists who simply jumped on the Puritan bandwagon when it appeared advantageous to them. Andrew was certainly in that category, and he had no reason to fear justice, since who would believe the word of the widow of a hated Loyalist over that of the man who had been the main supplier of the entire Parliamentary army?

"So what can he hope to gain by offering me honey?" she asked the solicitor.

"Your love, perhaps?" he said.

As time wore on, the formality of their visits began to dissipate somewhat. The boys had been wary of Andrew at first, seeing him only as the man who wanted to take their home away. Soon, however, Andrew's presence seemed to be making a positive impression on them, especially on Stuart. Andrew took time to question Stuart about the hunting and fishing prospects of the region, and Stuart responded with interest. Once when she was called away to deal with a problem in the kitchen, she returned to find Andrew and Stuart engrossed in a game of chess. She soon realized that at Stuart's very vulnerable age, he had needed a man in his life and sorely missed his father.

Benjamin, being younger, was less interested in Stuart's physical and intellectual pursuits, but eventually Andrew charmed him too, showing him new ways to place his wooden soldiers and telling him tales of how such and such a troop of English longbows had mown down a whole cavalry of Frenchmen in the Battle of Agincourt.

Judith also noticed with approval that he did not offer to take her hand again until his fourth visit. At that point, he merely took it in his and touched it to his forehead as he bowed.

By the tenth week, they had fallen into a bit of a routine, and Judith forgot to put on her gloves in anticipation of his visit. Thus, when she held out her hand, he took its nakedness as a sign of encouragement and kissed it. The touch of his lips on her bare flesh sent a chill through Judith's body of the kind she thought she had forgotten how to feel. As he picked up his head and their eyes met, she could feel her cheeks redden, but after holding her with his eyes for a split second only, he turned his gaze away and the conversation to safe pleasantries.

Nevertheless, a sort of bridge had been crossed. The gloves never reappeared, and the kisses continued, followed by longer and longer eye contact, with Judith cursing the whiteness of her skin, which could no more hide its blushing than the rose itself.

In the course of their visiting, Judith's year of mourning for Alex was finished, but as she had never ceased wearing all black since Richard's death, she continued. Not long afterward, though, she and the boys attended a special service for the anniversary of Richard's death, and the pain of their loss flooded back into them in full strength. After the service, the vicar's wife asked Judith if she had prepared a wardrobe to replace her widow's weeds, and when she expressed a desire to remain in mourning, as the loss of Richard was still so raw in her, the vicar told her that to do so would imply that she had not accepted God's will. "Remember, my child," he said, "the Lord giveth and the Lord taketh away. We must take up our cross and follow Him. We mustn't leave it and ourselves in the middle of the path to wallow in our own self-pity. You have two sons who need you. You do not have time for idle mourning."

His words shocked her. She had never thought about it in that way. She felt she would be disloyal to Richard's memory if she cast off her black garments, and she had nothing to replace them. Her former garments were much too large for her, her body thinned by worry and sorrow. They were also far too grand for her present financial state. She resolved to begin planning a more appropriate wardrobe the next day after Andrew's visit.

When he arrived, he was carrying a bundle in his arms that looked like cloth, rather than his usual sheaf of papers. "I have come with a gift," he said after he had greeted her. "I know that your period of mourning ended recently, but I also know that you do not have the money to buy the fine clothes you are accustomed to, and your black attire today tells me I was correct. I have taken the liberty of bringing you a garment worthy to be worn by the noble lady that you are."

With that he unrolled the bundle to reveal a dress of the finest emerald green silk, modestly and tastefully made, not showy, but with the exquisite workmanship Judith had always noticed about Andrew's own clothing.

"Oh, Mr. Selden, it's beautiful, but I cannot, I must not!" Judith protested.

"Please consider it a loan, just part of the mortgage. Surely the price of one dress will not make that much difference? If you and I are able to work something out, it will seem as nothing in the light of the entire debt."

Judith flinched at the mention of the debt, but the dress was magnificent, and she would have had a hard time justifying to herself the commissioning of such a garment.

"Then I accept it—as a loan. Thank you very much, Mr. Selden. You are very sensitive to my needs."

"Lady Chapman, you are my client. Whichever way this transaction goes, I stand to make a great deal of money. I can afford to be generous."

He sounded so professional and cold that Judith was taken aback. Like a slap in the face, his words reminded her that despite the unspoken relationship that had developed between them, or that she thought had developed, theirs was still a strictly professional association for him.

The following week, Judith wore the dress for his visit. He commented on how well she looked in it, and then got down to business. At one point in their conversation, Andrew requested a document that was in a large volume on a high shelf. As she went to retrieve it, Andrew, seeing the size of the volume and its height, went to assist her. As they both tugged on the heavy book, they both realized how close they were to each other. Embarrassed, she looked into his eyes and quickly away but then was unable to keep herself from looking back again. His eyes had a question in them, as if he was asking permission. This time she was unafraid to return his gaze, and in a minute his lips were on hers.

She did not remember ever having kissed a man so passionately, not even Richard. At first Andrew gave her short, almost pecking kisses, as though he was teasing, titillating her. It was a natural impulse for her to move closer to him, for more contact with his lips. That seemed to be the signal he was waiting for. He put his arms completely around her and pressed his lips more firmly on hers, but his mouth was never still. Then she felt his tongue on hers, and something in her went wild. She gave herself up to what she was feeling, and it was with the greatest of efforts that she pulled her mouth away from his and laid her hot cheek against his chest. She could hear his heart beating as well as her own.

He held her that way for a few moments and then released

her. "Judith," he said softly, his eyes searching hers. "Let's not do anything you'll regret later. I'll go now." He kissed her lightly one more time and then turned and left. She sank dazedly into the armchair in front of the bookcase.

"Mother, where's Mr. Selden?" The sound of Stuart's voice broke her stupor.

"What? Oh, he had to leave," she said. "He'll come again next week. Or perhaps before." At least that's what she hoped.

"Did he say anything about going hunting with me?" Stuart inquired, with knitted brow. He did not like to be disappointed when there was a hunting trip afoot.

"What? No, darling, he didn't, but I'm sure that's only because we had our minds on other things. I'm sure he won't forget if he made you a promise."

"Mother, are you all right?" Stuart, engrossed in his own concerns, had just noticed his mother's vacant look. "Nothing bad happened between you and Mr. Selden, did it? You're still friends, aren't you?"

"Oh, yes, dear, we're still very much friends," said Judith, finally regaining her composure. "The best of friends."

"That's good," said Stuart. "Things have gotten much nicer around here since Mr. Selden's been coming. I guess we all worried for nothing. He doesn't seem at all the kind of man who'd throw us out of our own house."

"No, he doesn't," said Judith. "You do like him very much, don't you, Stuart?"

"Yes, Mother, I do."

"And what about Benjy, does he like Mr. Selden too?"

"I guess so, but Mr. Selden doesn't play with him as much as Uncle Alex did. Sometimes Uncle Alex acted as though he was the same age as Benjy. But Mr. Selden is more like a grown-up, more like Father."

"Oh, you miss your father so, don't you, Stuart?" cried Judith, taking him in her arms. "So do I. Each day I realize how much more I miss him!"

"Yes, Mother, I miss him, but I'm trying to handle it as he would want me to. He wouldn't want us to be unhappy. The vicar says that when people are in heaven, all they want is for those they love to be as happy as possible. So that's what I'm trying to be. At first I felt guilty about going hunting and doing things with Mr. Selden that I used to do only with Father, but after the vicar told me that, I felt much better."

"Out of the mouths of babes…," Judith whispered, hugging her son again.

"What does that mean, Mother," asked Stuart?

"Oh, it's just a quotation from the Bible. Your speaking of the vicar reminded me of it."

"Oh. Well, all right, Mother. If I may, I'll go on out to the stables. I want to start exercising Prince to prepare him for the hunt. Mr. Selden says he's a fine stallion, as fine as the one he had as a boy."

Andrew did return in less than a week's time. When he entered the room as usual, Judith was afraid to look at him, afraid to reveal the excitement she was feeling. But after he had kissed her bare hand as usual, and the touch of his hand and his lips sent shivers through her entire body and the blood rushing to her cheeks, she had to look him in the eye. For a moment they drank each other in, and then she was in his arms again, all restraint gone.

"Judith," he said, finally, pulling away from her and searching her face, "these three days were a torment for me. I don't want to be away from you that long again, ever. Marry me, Judith!"

"Oh, Andrew," she said, "yes, yes, I will!"

The rest of that day and night was a blur for them. The boys were with their tutor all afternoon, and Judith sent them up to their rooms soon after supper, Andrew promising Stuart a hunting trip the next morning and Benjy a falconing lesson in the afternoon. Judith had had Colin prepare a bedroom for Andrew, once she knew he was staying, in one of the guest apartments where no one ever went, as it reputedly had a resident ghost. That was certainly a place no one would disturb. She led Andrew to it as soon as the boys had gone to bed, with strict instructions to Colin that he was to deal with all eventualities that might arise during the night. When Clara arrived in the morning to make Judith's bed, she was surprised to find that it had not been slept in.

As Andrew lay there with the sleeping Judith in his arms, he congratulated himself on his success. Everything he had planned had come to pass. With the Puritan government confiscating the property of known Royalists daily, he had not been at all sure that his claims to Chapman Hall would be upheld. He had had no trouble with the earlier foreclosures; there had still been too much confusion in the changeover of government. Now, however, Cromwell and his henchmen were well ensconced and looking about them for money to cover the war debts they owed to people like Andrew. He could have pressed his case in court, of course, but that would have taken time, time that he didn't want to waste, and lawyers that he didn't want to pay.

The Chapman estate was a really fine piece of property. Of all the estates to which Andrew had the right of foreclosure, it was one the biggest and most prosperous. Its original manor predated the Norman Conquest, and the property had passed, through marriage, into the hands of many noble families, each one adding its own prestige and power and buying (or stealing) land from its neighbors. Before the war, Richard Chapman had managed it well, and its fields and folds continued to produce abundantly. It was only the post-war glut that had put it within his grasp. Oh, how he wanted it! It was an estate to rival his father's, the jewel in the crown of properties he had been building since he left the army. He would be a country gentleman after all, but on his terms, not his father's!

And the best prize of all was Judith. He had made up his mind to marry her before he ever met her. The double claim of the mortgage and the marriage would give Cromwell's axe-men a hard time to take it from him. It had been his intention to force her into marriage to keep herself and her sons out of poverty, but he was immediately smitten by her and decided to woo her instead. That had been a much easier task than he anticipated as well, but he realized that he had indeed played his cards right. If he had rushed her, she would have felt herself duty-bound to reject him out of loyalty to her dead husband, but he won her gradually and let her mourning end decently before making his move. What had transpired between them all night was proof of both how lonely she had been and how ready she was to have another man in her life.

Her sons were another bonus for him as well as an aid to his courtship. Although his own mother had been somewhat aloof and he had spent more time with 'Lizbeth than with her, he had by now enough experience with women to know that the way to their hearts was through their children. If a man could win over the child, the mother would follow hard behind.

Besides, being with the boys was pleasant, especially with Stuart. He reminded Andrew of himself at the same age, except he was more reserved than Andrew had been, more mature. That came, he supposed, from Stuart's having had to deal with his father's death. It was clear that Stuart was as starved for a father as Judith was starved for a man's love. And Andrew found he had really missed the squire's pursuits of hunting, falconing, and so on while pursuing his self-made career. He liked returning to that part, at least, of the life of a country gentleman. He saw now that it was possible to live such a life without becoming boringly provincial as his father and many of his father's friends had been.

Judith sighed in her sleep and turned over. Andrew looked at her peaceful face on the pillow. She was completely different from Lucy, but every bit as beautiful. He would never feel he was getting second best. But where was Lucy? Did she have his child, or did she miscarry from the beating her father gave her when he found out she was pregnant? Where was she? He saw again her eager face as he kissed her that last time in the hayloft. How excited they both had been! They were going to run away together and live out their romantic dream in America, far away from the demands of society and custom.

Bitter gall welled up in Andrew's throat as he thought of the events of those days. He may not have found Lucy, but he had given Oliver Boyle what he deserved. Those poor, credulous soldiers. Andrew wondered what jail his father had them rotting in, or what colony enjoyed their hard labor. Maybe with the war over and things beginning to settle down, he could use his power and influence to find Lucy at last and perhaps see his child, if he had one..

Since Judith was a widow, she did not need her father's permission to marry, nor was there a question of dowry: legally, Andrew already owned all of her property. Moreover, because she had fallen so completely in love with him, she trusted him completely. When the time came to sign documents, it never even occurred to her to ensure a future for her sons. She signed without even reading the documents, much to the initial chagrin of her solicitor, who was soon pacified by a generous retainer from Andrew. Besides, it was obvious that Andrew loved her boys, especially Stuart. They were almost inseparable.

The wedding ceremony took place at the church door as before, but this time Judith wore the green silk dress that Andrew had brought to her. Even if she had wanted to wear her former white gown, which she didn't out of respect for Richard, she could no longer fit in it. Although she had lost a great deal of weight after Richard's death, her happiness with Andrew had enabled her to regain all she had lost and more. The extra pounds only made her more beautiful.

Her parents came from Waldby House along with her brothers and sister and their families. Richard's parents came as well to experience this bittersweet moment. Their sadness over the loss of their only child weighed heavily on them, but they were glad that their grandsons would still be able to live on the family lands and inherit the family titles. Sir William had verified that the small estate to which they had moved upon Judith and Richard's marriage was safe and that it had not been part of the mortgage.

Little changed after the wedding, since Andrew had pretty much been living at Chapman Hall since his proposal to Judith. He was away for days at a time seeing to his many business interests, but when he came home, he was happy to be with Judith and the boys and they to be with him. He always brought the boys presents, hunting or soldiering items for Stuart and books for Benjy. Judith was able to rehire the curate to tutor the boys, and their education advanced rapidly.

Judith and Andrew did well together. Andrew's money and knowledge ensured that the house and lands were cared for and productive. Judith and her boys were once more able to live as they had before the war and Richard's death. Still, the ghosts of Richard and Lucy haunted their marriage.

Stuart was especially happy because Andrew began training him for the military. Despite what had happened to his father, Stuart was always fascinated with war and the things of war, weapons, armor, horses, and strategy. Andrew had seen it all. In his position as a supplier to both sides in the Civil War, he had seen what worked and what didn't. By the time he was fifteen, Stuart had received better military training than almost anyone in his time. He grew to respect and even love Andrew. Once, Andrew let Stuart ride to Leeds with him for a business meeting. Stuart was impressed with the way Andrew dealt with the men at the meeting. He was friendly but firm and soon had them agreeing to all his demands. Because both Andrew and Stuart were blond, several men inquired whether Stuart was Andrew's son. This left Stuart with feelings of both pride and guilt.

Benjamin couldn't have been less interested. He wanted people or a book. He loved to talk and was a good listener as well. He befriended anyone who came along, from the highest lord to the lowest servant. They were all the same to him. The library at Chapman Hall was extensive, and Benjamin read every book he could lay his hands on.

Both boys again received tutoring from the local curate, who was quite pleased to add a stipend to his meager salary. Collections at churches were small after the war as people tried to put their lives back together. The schools most aristocratic boys attended were still in disarray from the war and were too far away for Judith. After losing Richard, she could not bear the thought of being separated from her boys.

Not being a farmer or having an aptitude for farming, Andrew nevertheless was a good judge of talent and hired an overseer for the estate who took the extra responsibility off the shoulders of Sir William and worked well with Giles, thus keeping the estate in the prosperous state in which Richard had left it. The fields continued to be ripe and fruitful, and the barns and stables and sheepcotes were full. After a period of low prices, the estate began to make money again. Andrew could be a hard man, but when people served him well, he paid them well, and the employees at Chapman Hall were a happy lot. It seemed that everything Andrew touched turned into money.

Andrew was a good husband and stepfather, and Judith was happy again. Their lovemaking continued to be satisfying, and, always an apt student, she was beginning to learn about Andrew's business and to respect and admire him for his administrative acumen. This is not to say that she did not miss Richard. The young love they had shared and the early lives of her boys were often the subjects of her reveries. Her relationship with Andrew was a grownup relationship, and it was good, but sometimes she yearned for the spontaneity and innocence that she had enjoyed with Richard and that the war had taken away.

Judith was thirty-three when she and Andrew married, still able to but not likely to become pregnant. Relying on this unlikelihood, doing nothing to prevent pregnancy, and deep down wanting to have Andrew's child, after about a year and a half of marriage, she conceived.

The pregnancy was very hard on her. She had morning sickness almost from the beginning. After her remarriage, Judith had begun the project of decorating the east wing of the house that she and Richard had started and was enjoying selecting fabrics and furniture, but soon, as in her previous pregnancies, the demands of her pregnancy made it impossible for her to climb all the stairs. This time, however her debility happened earlier in the pregnancy. Andrew felt impatient with her condition, never having experienced pregnancy before, but he was pragmatic enough to realize quickly that she needed support more than anything else, and he gave it to her, because when she was happy, everyone else, including him, was happier.

Several weeks before nine months were up, Judith's water broke. A rider was dispatched to summon Judith's mother from Waldby House, the midwife was called in, and about twelve hours later, Basil was born. He was a small, sickly baby, but Andrew doted on him, although every time he held Basil in his arms, he thought of that other child, the one he might never know, who might never have seen the light of day as far as he knew. That would bring him to thoughts of his beloved Lucy—softness when he thought of the feel of her in his arms and anger at his father for separating them.

Judith seemed to recover from the birth, but in truth, there was sickness inside her. Before she was even allowed to get out of bed, she developed "milk leg," which was then thought to be the result of "bad" milk coming into her breasts but is now known to be the beginning of a blood clot, caused by being forced to endure the long "lying in" period thought to be healthy for new mothers. She insisted on breast-feeding Basil herself, as she had done with Stuart and Benjy, but she never stopped bleeding after the delivery, and by the time Basil was two months old, she was a shadow of her former buxom self.

Andrew was so busy with the estate, his other business affairs, playing with Basil, teaching Stuart, and guiding Benjy's reading that he hardly noticed Judith during this time. She had remained in bed for almost two months after the delivery, as was the custom of the time, and when they resumed sex again, her breasts were still large from lactating, so he didn't really notice how thin she was getting. Clara had tried to speak to him about Judith several times, but he was too busy to listen.

When Judith requested a special gathering to celebrate Basil's first three months on earth, Andrew was only too happy to oblige. They invited Judith's family and Richard's and all the area folk of their class. Colin and Clara and the rest of the household staff bustled about for days before, getting the house ready and the food and drink prepared.

Judith decided to make the party really special by wearing the green silk dress that had been her first big gift from Andrew and that she had worn for their wedding. When she put it on, it hung on her as though she were a child playing dress-up with her mother's clothes. She pressed Clara into service taking it in, and she did wear it, but it looked all distorted on her emaciated body. Her mother and Andrew were the most shocked by her appearance. For the first time in months, he really looked at her and was dismayed at the circles under her eyes and the pallor of her skin.

After the banquet, he called her mother aside, and they decided to speak to her about getting a wet nurse for Basil and having a doctor come to look at her. Andrew was leery of doctors, having seen their mismanagement of battle injuries and illnesses, but he let himself be persuaded. He couldn't bear to see his once-beautiful wife in that condition.

Judith initially opposed the idea of a wet nurse but eventually yielded to the pressure of her loved ones. She had secretly feared for some time that Basil was not flourishing on her milk. She did not demur at all at the suggestion of a doctor. She knew something was wrong but hesitated to say it. She had done so well with her two previous deliveries that she couldn't face the fact that this one was different, even with the same midwife.

They found a young peasant woman in the village who had just given birth but whose baby had died the day after. She was given a cottage on the estate and was allowed to have her other two young children with her. Her husband already worked as a laborer on the estate. Andrew paid her well, and she was happy with the arrangement.

Basil seemed to thrive on the milk from this healthier source. It made Judith sad at the same time that it relieved her. The doctor who was summoned declared Judith to be suffering from simple malnutrition and prescribed extra food. This seemed to work, at least at first, and Judith began to put on a few pounds and to have increased energy. While Basil was with the wet nurse, she was able to spend time with the other boys, time they would treasure in years to come.

Unfortunately, the doctor's treatment of Judith was no match for what was actually inside her, and within a week after Basil's party, she developed what felt like a charley horse in her left leg. Soon the leg was swollen and tender. The skin on her leg was mottled red and blue and felt warm.

She took to her bed again, but it was too late. Unbeknownst to any of them, the blood clot that had developed during her confinement had broken off as a result of the increased activity of her preparations for the party and was making its way to her lung.

Soon her breathing became painful, and her chest ached with each deep breath or cough. Every time she tried to get up to lessen the coughing, she became light-headed and in danger of fainting. Then she began to cough up blood.

Between coughs, she had Clara summon the family. Her parents were still at Chapman Hall, having decided to wait to see how Basil fared with the wet nurse. Judith was able to stop coughing only long enough to kiss her loved ones goodbye, after which she appeared to have fainted. She never awakened.

Judith's death changed Andrew. He cursed fate, which had once again deprived him of the woman he loved. All the softness that had entered his life with Judith began to evaporate, replaced by the hardness that had made him such a force during the war.

Only Basil brought out the best in his father. He looked like Judith, and when Andrew was with him, he showed the child the same tenderness he had always displayed with Judith.

The older boys didn't fare as well. Just when they needed Andrew the most in dealing with their mother's death, he began to pull away from them, especially from Stuart, who looked more like Richard. Andrew had never had that close a relationship with Benjy because of his bookish ways, but he and Stuart had had a bond of masculine interests.

Stuart was fifteen and needed a man in his life, but Andrew was no longer available to him. He didn't understand why this man who had seemed to care about him suddenly didn't want him around. Andrew had seemed proud that people thought Stuart was his son. Had he misread all of that? In his grief, he reached out to his grandfather Waldby, but the Waldbys lived three days away. His uncles Geoffrey and Stephen lived equally far away and were busy with their young families and with rebuilding their lives after the war. He was ambiguous about his grandfather Chapman, feeling that the relationship he had had with Andrew made him somehow disloyal to Richard. He began to spend time with the overseer of the estate. This man was good at his work but somewhat uncomfortable having an upper-class teenager underfoot all the time. He had sons of his own, but they were young, and he had never dealt with teenagers before.

Nevertheless, Stuart was pleasant and eager, and he asked good questions, so the overseer tolerated him and explained as well as he could all that was going on throughout the estate. Since Stuart had already learned so much about farming from Sir William during Richard's absence during the war, Stuart soaked it all up like a sponge, and it stood him in good stead years later. It wasn't much, but it was all he had.

As grief gave way to hardness, Andrew began to think about Basil's future. Although he had many other properties, including his father's, which had come to him upon his father's death despite his renunciation of his family, the Chapman estate was valuable and productive property, and he wanted Basil to have it. He knew Basil would inherit no land from Judith's family. Her dowry had already gone to Richard and been lost in the war. Her brothers would have all the Waldby property.

So he hired an army of lawyers and began the process of divesting Stuart and Benjy of their inheritance from their father. Judith had not been in her grave an entire year when his goal was accomplished and he sent the boys to live with Richard's parents.

Andrew deceived the boys at first. "I need for you boys to spend some time with your grandparents," he told them. "I need to be away for an extended period of time, and I need for Clara and Colin to focus on Basil since he's so much younger."

"But Andrew," Stuart protested, "we're old enough to look after ourselves. We don't need Clara and Colin."

"I know you're growing up, Stuart," returned Andrew, but I'll feel better if I know you're under your grandparents' supervision. When I was your age, I was always trying to circumvent my parents' wishes, and Colin and Clara are pushovers when it comes to both you and Benjy."

"What if I promised to do just as they said?" continued Stuart. "Don't you trust me? Besides, you know Benjy won't do anything except read books. That's all he ever does. I love my grandparents, but they're old and boring. I want to stay here."

"No, Stuart. I have made my decision. You must go to your grandparents. That's final," said Andrew.

The look on Andrew's face told Stuart to back off, and he did. He sadly gathered up a few belongings, put them in his saddlebags, and rode to the Chapmans' after assuring himself that Benjy would follow later, accompanied by his friend the curate.

The Chapmans had not been informed that they were to have visitors, but they were very glad to see Stuart and then Benjy, and they set about making the boys comfortable. Sophia had her cook prepare their favorite dishes, and Sir William assigned each a stall for his horse.

At first things went well. Stuart spent time with Sir William on his rounds of the farms and barns, during which time Sir William continued Stuart's education in the raising of sheep. For the first time, Benjy had time to spend in the elder Chapmans' library and found much to enjoy.

Then the letter came, and with it a large wagon containing everything the boys owned and everything, as far as they could tell, that had been Richard's.

Sir William and Sophia were more than happy to have their grandsons but were aghast at Andrew's perfidy. They hired lawyers themselves to try to overturn what Andrew had done, but his money had secured him airtight possession of their former estate, and they could do nothing.

It was Colin himself who had driven the wagon with the boys' possessions. "If it weren't for Basil," Colin told the Chapmans, "Clara and I would leave right now and go back to the Waldbys. But Clara says we can't leave little Basil with nobody to see about him, so we'll be there if you need us."

Stuart and Benjy understood little of the legal maneuverings around them. All they knew was that life as they had known it was forever gone. The little stability they still felt after Judith's death was denied them as they were forced to leave the home in which they were born and in which they had spent their entire short lives.

Benjy, as usual, was able to give words to his anger and disappointment, but Stuart just became more reserved than ever, keeping to himself whenever possible. He and Benjy often visited their parents' graves, but this gesture brought no comfort to Stuart.

The Chapmans were able to continue the boys' education after a fashion, engaging the same curate as tutor, but Stuart's military education ground to a halt. When the Chapmans were young, a boy of Stuart's age would have been sent to the home of a relative to be trained, but the war had changed all that, and besides, Stuart did not want to leave Benjy. They remained with their grandparents for two years. To give the devil his due, Andrew did provide each of the boys with a small sum of money to finance his entry into whatever field he chose, but it was a pittance compared with what he had taken away.

By early 1656, the Puritans had been in power for nearly seven years and had begun to relax slightly their strictures against the Church of England. Some of the seminaries were beginning to reopen, including the one at York. After having observed Benjy at close quarters for two years, the Chapmans were by no means surprised when Benjy asked if he could go there. They consulted with the curate, who was probably Benji's closest friend, and with the vicar, both of whom had had ample opportunity to observe the young man, and they concurred that the cloth was a good choice for Benji. There was little else for someone in his situation. An impoverished gentleman had few opportunities. He could have, of course, helped his grandfather with the small farm that remained on the estate they had kept, but that would not allow him the lifestyle his parents would have wanted, and his Waldby grandparents, with more children, had no land to spare for him. Having lost his father in war, he was staunchly opposed to anything military and had never been interested in it anyway.

Accordingly, the Chapmans were relieved of some worry about their younger grandson and gladly acceded to his request. Churchmen often rose to positions of great wealth and power, and Benji, they believed, had what it took to do so. They used the money Andrew had provided to secure him a place and provide for him during his studies, and Benjy began the journey toward becoming an Anglican priest.

The choice was a good one, and he thrived. His letters to his

Chapman grandparents and Stuart were frequent and chatty, full of anecdotes about his teachers and his fellow seminarians. Since his Waldby relatives lived fewer than forty miles from York, he was able to see them often and regaled his Chapman relatives with accounts of the antics of Goeff's children and his time with Sally's daughters and their friends.

He loved his theology classes, but the pomp and ceremony of the liturgical celebrations were the most compelling for him, and he longed for the return of the traditional rituals of the pre-Puritan Church of England. He described in the most minute detail every inch of York Cathedral, every chapel, tomb, statue, and niche.

Stuart, now alone with his grandparents, began to think of his own future. He had learned so much about farming during his father's absence and was so helpful to his grandfather that the Chapmans wished he might join his grandfather in researching and sheep breeding, but they knew that was a vain hope. Although Stuart had the aptitude, the estate was too small to yield the kind of living a young man of his status should have. They reluctantly came to the conclusion that the army was probably his only choice, but because of Richard's death, they hated putting another loved one's life in danger.

The thought of joining Oliver Cromwell's New Model Army was repugnant to Stuart, but he had wanted to be a soldier all his life, and he longed to try his hand at practicing what he had learned from his father and uncles and from Andrew. Despite the family's Royalist leanings, with Andrew's help and money, he was able to secure a low-level commission. Although there was not yet a standing army in England, Cromwell had maintained a small number of troops to deal with Royalist uprisings, which had continued even after the king's execution. Most who had fought during the war were eager to return to their homes and pre-war occupations, but a number remained to maintain order in the Commonwealth.

Dealing with his Puritan superiors, however, was unpleasant for him, and the name Stuart earned him many an insult. Thus when an opportunity came to go to Virginia to protect the colonists from the "savages," as the natives were then called, and their French and Dutch allies, he jumped at the chance. At this time, the French were still mostly confined to what would later become Canada, but during the war when the English colonies were poorly defended, the French had begun to make inroads into the English colonies and to befriend the natives.

The colony of Virginia had acknowledged the authority of Parliament five years earlier, but the colonists themselves had in reality remained loyal to the monarchy, even after Parliament sent a fleet to force them to submit. Thus numerous Royalists had fled to Virginia after Charles was beheaded. Many with military experience joined what were called "independent companies," each composed of fifty to a hundred soldiers from Britain, with officers, and financed usually by a well-to-do colonist. Their job was to defend the colony and to support offensive campaigns.

In 1655, the Dutch had taken control of New Sweden, in what would later become the state of Delaware, and had fought the Peachtree War against the Susquehannock tribe and their allies. In that same year, Lord Baltimore, the Lord Proprietor of the Maryland colony, had led colonial troops against the Puritan settlers of the northern colonies. Both events had prompted the Virginia colonists to seek more military resources.

Stuart bore the ocean voyage beautifully, the first of many he was to make. He liked the sea so well that he was tempted to abandon army life for the navy, but since he had committed himself to be a land warrior, he threw himself into the military life of the colony with youthful gusto. His company was garrisoned in a fort near the coast, and he greatly enjoyed being near the water for the first time in his young life.

Although there was strife between the British and the natives, Stuart met and came to know many of them. The Algonquian tribes lived on Virginia's coastal plain and were farmers. Having grown up on a farm, Stuart was able to relate to them and to relate to their challenges and successes. He was able to master enough of their language and they of his to exchange stories and to compare their growing of maize to his family's oats and barley. He was surprised and amused that they considered the British, who seldom bathed, to be uncivilized, as they themselves bathed daily. He gave careful thought to their demand for balance in life, and he regretted that his countrymen were jeopardizing their way of life by taking their land for tobacco plantations. He could see why they were hostile. Nevertheless, as he was a soldier, he knew that he would fight them if he had to. He remembered his mother's stories about his father's reluctance to go to war against his neighbors. He now knew exactly what his father had been feeling.

He wrote regularly to all his relatives in England, and they to him, but the ocean crossing took so long that he went for months without hearing from anyone. Those were lonely times for him, but he bore them with resignation. When the letters did come, he felt once more that he belonged.

After a year and a half, he got permission to return to England for a visit, serving as a guard on a supply ship, and his reunions with both sides of his family were wonderful. He was shocked, however, at how much all four of his grandparents had aged. During his absence, when he thought of them, he thought of their younger selves, the way they had been when he was a child. Now he dreaded that when he left once more for Virginia, he might never see them again. They had already outlived the usual lifespan of the time, but they had always been well fed and healthy, and despite the troubles they had faced as a result of the war, they were still in good mental states and more or less mobile, though by no means the way they had been before.

Sir William still saw to his sheep, but he had more hired help than before. Two of his hands were actually men who had been in Richard's regiment and were glad to relocate where work was available. They were full of praise for Richard, and Stuart greatly enjoyed their anecdotes of their military life with his father, though they reminded him of how much he had lost.

Sir William was proud to show Stuart the newest in the flock. The young sheep had beautiful, long wool, the kind that would be great for spinning, and it would be even longer by shearing time. Stuart noted that the wool was much better than that of the sheep in Virginia, which had not had the benefit of Sir William's research.

"Look at that old man," Sir William gestured. "Remember him?"

"Is that old Charlie?" asked Stuart.

"Yes, indeed," said Sir William. "Still the best ram in the riding."

"Does he still try to butt everybody?" asked Stuart. "I have dodged those horns more than once!"

"Yes, he does," chuckled Sir William. "A gent came from Halifax the other day to see about buying a few of old Charlie's offspring, and old Charlie nearly ran him off the property! He's still up to his old tricks."

"Grandfather, why did you name him Charlie?" Stuart asked.

"After the king, of course," said Sir William. "If only the king had been as good at his job as old Charlie! Your father tried to tell me, but I wouldn't listen." A tear formed in Sir William's eye as he said this.

"What do you mean?" asked Stuart.

"Your father really did not want to fight for the king, Stuart. He felt the king was making unwise decisions. He was right, of course, but at the time, I couldn't see it. He foresaw what would be the ultimate result, but he went on anyway because I made him feel it was his duty. My foolishness will haunt me to the end of my days!"

Stuart was stunned, but he tried to comfort his grandfather. "I'm sure my father did what he himself thought was right, Grandfather. You should not blame yourself."

"I wish I could believe that, Stuart," said Sir William sadly.

For her part, Sophia mostly sat and sewed. "I have done all I can to this house," she told Stuart, "and now that you and Benji are gone, no one around here really needs me, so I spend my time sewing for poor children. The war left so many penniless that there are poor orphans in rags everywhere. It's the least I can do."

Stuart's heart went out to his grandmother, bereft of her only child and with his children so far away. Benji went to visit every few months, but it was never enough.

At Waldby House, Sir Henry used a cane daily and seldom rode his horse. He made an exception to ride around the property with Stuart and let him admire the sheep and the crops. He was one of Sir William's best customers for sheep, and he reminisced about his visits to Chapman Hall. Geoff and Stephen had relieved him of all his chores on what was left of the Waldby property after the family had paid their debts to Andrew. They had been more circumspect and less generous than Richard, not continuing to pay the families of dead soldiers, so there was more left, and Stephen and Alex had not been in the war long enough to owe too much. "I'm so lucky to have my boys here to help me," he told Stuart. "Getting old is not for cowards, boy. Do all you can while you're young so you won't have regrets later."

Stuart promised he would take that advice. He had never been as close to Sir Henry as to Sir William, and seeing his grandfather now made him wish he could spend more time with him.

Diana remained her usual fluttery self, though she fluttered much more slowly. She was kept busy enjoying her latest grandchildren and her garden. Geoff had a girl and a boy now, and Stephen's new wife was expecting, so Diana had much to occupy her time. "That little Genevieve is such an opinionated young lady," she told Stuart. "I feel as though I'm dealing with your mother again. Judith always had a mind of her own. What I wouldn't give to have her back!" Diana said wistfully.

Those words were like a knife in Stuart's heart, reopening the wounds of losing his mother. He wondered if that pain ever went away.

Nancy, who had mostly retired during Stuart's absence, was pressed back into service for the visit, and she delighted Stuart by preparing dishes that Judith had loved and sharing stories of Judith with him.

Geoff now had a few streaks of grey in his dark hair, and he seemed thinner than Stuart had remembered, perhaps having lost some of the muscle bulk he had acquired during his years as a soldier. He had not only become reconciled to being a farmer but seemed to love it. "I guess it was in my blood after all," he told Stuart. "It's a lot of work, but when you see that pile of wool ready for market and those crops in sheaves drying, it's very satisfying."

Stephen concurred. He had always been a farmer at heart, and having his brother as a partner suited him very well. Stuart liked Stephen's wife, whom Stephen had married during Stuart's absence. She was just a few years older than Stuart and very dainty, but she had a good attitude and seemed to be bearing the vicissitudes of pregnancy philosophically.

Sally had put aside her widow's weeds long before and was being courted by one of the Overtons from down the coast. Alex's land was valuable property, and numerous suitors had made themselves available over the years since Alex's death, but Sally had been smarter than Judith had been and had established legal protections for herself and her daughters. The Overtons were wealthy Puritans who seemed willing to agree to her terms.

Benji came up from York, and Stuart had a pleasant and amusing time with his little brother. Benji was seventeen, with a good start of a beard, dark like his mother's hair. Stuart was a bit jealous, as his was still somewhat sparse. Although his hair wasn't blond like Richard's, but rather medium brown, he had inherited the Chapman dearth of facial and body hair.

Diana and Sally made sure Stuart met all the eligible young ladies of the area, and Stuart roared with laughter at Benji's descriptions of each one after every party. Benji seemed to be drawn to one of Alex's nieces, and Stuart had to agree that she would probably make a fine vicar's wife. Stuart did not find a girl who interested him, though, much to Diana's disappointment. After the harsh realities of the Virginia frontier, these girls seemed shallow and sheltered.

While Stuart was in West Yorkshire, he made a point of going to Chapman Hall. Andrew was away, but he had a nice visit with Clara and Colin. They made him promise to write to them. Neither could read, but they could get the curate or the vicar to read the letters for them. He also spent a little time with Basil, but Basil, being barely four, didn't really understand that Stuart was his half brother, though he was a friendly child, and Stuart liked him. He had been so small when Stuart had left that he didn't have the personality he now displayed. Even as little as he was, he looked so much like Judith that it brought tears to Stuart's eyes.

Since Andrew was not there, Stuart was free to roam the house and enjoy memories of his childhood, which now seemed so, so long ago. Andrew had apparently spent so little time in the house that he had changed nothing in Richard's solar, not even the hangings with the Chapman coat of arms. Stuart stayed in that room so long that Colin felt the need to go and check on him.

"I'm fine, Colin," Stuart replied to Colin's concerned questions. "I feel my father's spirit here, that's all. I hope he'll always be here where I can come and visit him."

"We'll try to make sure that can happen," Colin replied. "I don't know how, but we'll try."

Stuart also rode all around the estate, reliving experiences with both of his parents as he and Judith and Benjy had done after Richard's death. It was a bittersweet time for him. So much was the same, yet so much had changed!

Finally his leave was up, and after stopping in York to let Benji share his new home and environment, Stuart again set sail for Virginia. He wondered wistfully when he would get to return, if ever.

Doted on by Clara, who missed his mother greatly, Basil overcame his initial sickliness and became a healthy toddler. He was so young when Judith died and when his brothers left that he did not miss them. His wet nurse stayed with him until he was able to drink from a cup; after that, as far as he knew, Clara was his mother. His only playmates were the children of the workers on the estate, and he was not lonely. Sometimes, in the evenings, Andrew would play with him, too. He was a happy child.

At the time when Andrew and his lawyers were hard at work depriving the Chapman boys of their father's estate, Andrew was forty-four years old. In the seventeenth century, a person who lived past the age of sixty was rare, and most died much younger, although the aristocracy often lived beyond that as their diets and lifestyles were more healthful than those of the majority of the population.

Still, a death, especially of one as young as Judith, always reminds people around it of their own mortality, and Andrew was no exception. While he had lawyers in his pay, he had them draw up a will. He left all of his possessions to Basil and his descendants. At the recommendation of his main solicitor, a man named Pearce, he also added that if Basil died without issue, Andrew's estate would go to his child with Lucy Digby, if such a child existed, and to the descendants of that child. Andrew refused to think beyond that eventuality.

All seemed well with Andrew and Basil for the next couple of years. Andrew threw himself into his business ventures, not even taking a mistress or availing himself of the prostitutes who reached out to him when he walked the city streets.

He was often away for weeks at a time.

During that time, Basil missed his father but accepted his lot, not knowing any other. However, once when Andrew was to be away for over a month, Clara asked permission to take Basil to Waldby House to visit his grandparents. Diana had sent messages through the Chapmans, begging for a visit from Basil since Sir Henry was too arthritic to travel the three days' distance to Chapman Hall. They sorely missed seeing their grandson, and Stuart's visit and news of the Waldbys had made Clara want to see her own family.

Andrew agreed and made provisions for the trip. He insisted that Colin stay behind to look after the house, but he sent one of his young employees to ride beside the carriage.

Basil loved the trip. Even though he was just a little past four, he was delighted with everything he saw and heard, and the Waldby relatives who housed them on the way spoiled him rotten.

Diana's heart was full as she watched the carriage drive up in front of the house, her thoughts going back to that day so many years before when Richard and Judith had first met. When Basil stepped out and Judith's face looked up at her out of his, she dissolved.

"What's the matter with Grandmother?" Basil asked Clara, frowning.

Before Clara could answer, Diana had him in her arms, kissing him all over, tears streaming down her cheeks.

"Nothing's the matter with Grandmother now that you're here!" she cried. "I'm crying because I'm so happy to see you."

This worked for Basil, and he was soon exploring his surroundings as only a curious four-year-old boy can do.

The month passed much too fast for all the adults involved. Diana and Henry were loath to let Basil go, their final connection to Judith. Clara was reveling in visiting the region of her birth and all her relatives, including Nancy, who still occasionally cooked for the Waldbys even though she was getting on in age. "Only two of them left here now," she told Clara, "not too much for me to handle, and it's not every day."

Over the month, Basil had made friends with all the children whose parents worked Henry's fields and stables and was heartbroken when one day his favorite playmate, Ethan, the grandson of Clara's older sister, didn't come with his father.

"I'm so sorry, Master Basil," Ethan's father said, "but Ethan is sick. Maybe he'll be able to come with me tomorrow."

But Ethan never came back, his sickness worsening over the rest of Basil's stay.

Basil took it in stride, as he did everything, and played with the other children, but he missed Ethan.

The day that Basil and Clara left, Basil was cranky, which was unusual for him but understandable since he had to leave a place where he had had so much fun and had been treated so well.

He remained cranky for the entire trip, and even seeing his father and his friends from home did not improve his attitude. Andrew cursed Clara for letting him be spoiled and swore he would never allow another such trip.

Within less than six months, it was obvious that Basil was really ill. He began coughing uncontrollably for minutes at a time, and soon he was coughing up blood, as his mother had done. A letter from the Waldbys having confirmed that Ethan had consumption, a doctor was brought in for Basil. It was not the same doctor who had treated Judith, as Andrew could not stand the sight of the man who had let his beloved wife die, but as was typical of the time, the new doctor's treatments were equally fruitless. Basil was forced to drink a "cordial" of the juices of roasted mutton, veal, and capon together with a little orange juice.

For only the second time in his life, Andrew let love overpower greed. He turned the running of his businesses over to his employees and sat by Basil's side constantly, bathing his fevered brow with cool water and feeding him broth when Basil could swallow it, hardly sleeping at all himself. The poor little fellow hung on for almost a year, but finally he passed away in great pain, coughing up blood with almost every breath.

His death was the last straw for Andrew. He called in his lawyers and set them on a quest, to find his child by Lucy. They advised him that in case there was no such child, he needed to decide who else would receive his money and property upon his death. Although he blamed the Waldbys for Basil's death and wanted nothing to do with them or theirs, he had to admit that the only other person to whom he had ever felt close was Stuart. Thus he allowed the lawyers to name Stuart as his heir should he have no child by Lucy or should that child have no descendants.

Part VI

As the days of Sun Woman's pregnancy drew to a close, she was the subject of much gossip within the village. Everyone wondered whether her child would look Indian or European. No one was certain, least of all Sun Woman herself, whether Sun Woman had already conceived when Jeremy raped her or if the child was Jeremy's. The outcome would not normally have been a problem for the villagers, as they often adopted European orphans, but the memory of the English raid was still strong in their minds, and feeling ran high against anything English.

Finally the day came, and Sun Woman delivered a healthy baby girl. She had straight black hair and dark blue eyes, but all babies had blue eyes. The village gave a collective sigh of relief, and the little girl, who was named Sun Child after her mother, was taken into the hearts of her people. She was a shy little thing, deferring to everyone, not selfish, even at a young age, with the meager, homemade toys her grandparents made for her.

By the time she was two, however, it became obvious to everyone that her hair, though still quite dark, was going to be very curly and that her eyes were lightening into a true blue. Her skin became lighter almost by the day. Nevertheless, she had been accepted, and no one said a word, though they sometimes gossiped among themselves, calling her White Water instead of Sun Child.

As she aged, Sun Child continued her shy, unassuming behavior, always obedient to her parents, helpful to others. By the time she reached her teens, she had blossomed into a beauty.

At that point, some of the other girls began to be jealous of the way the eyes of every young man sought out Sun Child whenever she went by. Older men commented to their wives about what a good wife she would make, she who was both beautiful and docile. Through no fault of her own, Sun Child soon had many enemies among the female population of the village.

A drought followed by a flood ruined the village's crops of corn and beans the year that Sun Child turned fourteen. That loss sealed

Sun Child's fate. When misfortune occurs, people always look for a scapegoat, and they chose her. The women convinced the men that the harboring of an enemy within the village was what had caused the crop failures. A delegation was chosen to meet with Sun Woman and her husband and demand that Sun Child be sent away, "back to the English where she belongs," they said.

Sun Woman was beside herself with anxiety for her child. Her husband was pulled in both directions. On the one hand, he had come to love Sun Child as his own, but on the other, he felt very heavily the responsibility for the well being of the village. If his daughter was indeed the problem, then he owed it to his neighbors to do something about her.

The solution arrived in the form of a trader, Francis Cooper, who came to the village to exchange the staple goods the villagers so badly needed for animal pelts they had cured over the previous winter. As he was negotiating with the villagers, Sun Child walked by, carrying a pot of water on her head. When Cooper saw her, he was struck, like everyone else, by her beauty, and inquired as to who she was. At that point, neither Sun Woman nor her husband was nearby to be offended, so one of the women, who had at one time been a prisoner of the English and had learned their language, told the story. "Don't you want her?" the woman asked. "She's half English, and she's as mild as a doe. I, for one, would be glad to get rid of her." She proceeded to tell Cooper how Sun Child's presence in the village had ruined their crops.

Cooper's mental wheels began to turn. He was almost forty, and women in the colonies were scarce. Here was a girl who was at least half English, and a beauty to boot. She was in no position to complain about the meager cabin in which he lived, and if she had children by him, they would be three-quarters white. He could always tell people she was Welsh, and no one would know better. Accordingly, he asked the woman to take him to the girl's home.

Through the woman, he made offers of food staples and other goods to Sun Child's parents. Although the things he offered amounted to little of what he actually possessed, they were impressive to the couple. He told them that for an Englishman, it was normal to expect that the girl's parents would provide her with a dowry to take into her marriage, but that he considered Sun Child's beauty to be enough of a dowry for him. He promised that he would love her for the rest of his life and take the best of care of her, providing her with a beautiful permanent home in which she would reign as queen. This last was an incomprehensible concept to the couple, but he made it sound very fine, and they were quite taken with him. They asked for time to discuss it, and he said he would return the following day.

Sun Woman was impressed but reluctant to give up her beloved daughter. Her husband was in favor of it, reminding her that they would still see her every time the trader came to the village and that they could go to her home sometimes, too. It did not occur to either of them to demur on the basis of Sun Child's age, as the marriage of a fourteen-year-old girl was quite common.

Goading them along was the woman who had helped with the negotiations. She pointed out that the longer they kept Sun Child, the more antagonistic the village would become toward her, especially if the following year's crop was not good. She told them of the fine English lifestyle she had observed while a prisoner and assured them that they were actually doing their daughter a favor. Soon they were persuaded.

That night, they called Sun Child to them and told her the news. She was incredulous at first and then heartbroken when they told her for the first time the truth about her conception. She who had always felt so loved and affirmed suddenly felt like a stranger. Even her mother, whom she had always adored, seemed like someone foreign. Silent tears began to flow, but she nodded her acceptance and went off to her pallet, where she cried herself to sleep.

The next day when Cooper returned, he brought her English clothes to wear, and the woman who spoke English dressed her hair like that of an Englishwoman. The clothes were hot and confining, and the shoes pinched her feet. She never wore anything on her feet in warm weather and only soft deerskin in the cold months. Being a "fine English lady" did not seem appealing at all. Nevertheless, being the malleable creature that she was, she accepted her new clothing without complaint.

Although Cooper had been in the village all the day before, Sun Child had not really looked at him, so it was a surprise when she did so. He looked so old—older than her father, and his face was all bumpy with smallpox scars. His reddish-brown hair hung in rattails to his shoulders, and he looked and smelled as if he had never bathed. Sun Child was repulsed. She looked at her mother pleadingly, but her mother's smile told her that she would find no help from that quarter. It was a sad and uncomfortable young girl who walked away from the village that day to a fate that she feared and quietly rejected.

The couple walked for many hours. Cooper had a horse, but it carried only his wares. Sun Child was accustomed to walking many miles at a time, but not in English shoes, and her feet were painful and blistered very quickly.

Cooper chattered at her the whole time they walked. She understood nothing of what he said unless he specifically pointed to something and said its name, after which he pointed to her and she repeated it, brokenly at first, but better as time went on. She quickly learned that she was "Martha." She had no idea if that was a name or simply a word for "girl" or "woman." She assumed it didn't mean "wife," as there had been no marriage ceremony.

Each time they sat down to rest, Cooper pulled food from his pack and shared it with her. It tasted strange, but she was hungry, so she ate, even though her stomach began hurting almost immediately. Each time they rested, she removed her shoes and stockings and let the air caress her sore feet. Whenever they stopped at a stream or lake, she hiked up her voluminous skirts and waded in, letting the cool water soothe her.

The third time she did that, though, Cooper waded in with her, pulled her into deeper water, and reached his hand under her skirt, touching her private parts, cupping one of her breasts with his other hand. Then he pulled her against him and kissed her, thrusting his tongue into her mouth. When she fought back and pushed him under water, he slapped her and yelled at her. Not understanding, she ran as fast as she could out of the water and never went in again, although her feet screamed for relief. At least he smelled better after his dunking.

The sun was disappearing behind the trees when they finally reached Cooper's cabin. It was made of logs and had only one room, with a stone fireplace along one wall and a single window on another. A wooden bedstead stood in the corner farthest from the door. A small wooden table and two chairs completed the furnishings, except for several trunks that lined the wall with the door. Large nails jutted from the other walls in various places, and from them hung items of clothing. On the raised hearth were a few sooty metal pots and utensils and a few logs of cooking wood. The remains of a small fire still glowed faintly. The table held a tallow lamp and a couple of place settings consisting of pewter plates, stoneware cups, and roughly made spoons and knives.

As she was looking around her new dwelling, Cooper chattered along, occasionally pointing to something and saying its name. Sun Child obediently repeated each word as well as she could. Exhausted, she let herself drop to the floor and removed the horrid shoes and stockings. The cool dirt of the floor felt wonderful. She also realized that she was hungry. She made signs of putting food into her mouth and chewing it so Cooper would see.

Laughing, he went to one of the trunks and brought out salted turkey meat, which he put on one of the plates on the table. He cut off a piece and put it on the other plate and sat in a chair, motioning Sun Child to do likewise. It was her first time to sit in a chair.

She ate some of the meat, and it wasn't bad, but it soon made her thirsty. She picked up one of the cups and made a gesture as if drinking. Cooper laughed again and led her outside, carrying a wooden bucket that he picked up from beside the fireplace. The house was on a slight hill, and Cooper walked about fifty yards down and to the right. There a spring bubbled up under a blanket of leaves. He began to clean the leaves away, with her help, and soon was able to dip the bucket in and bring it up filled with cool, clear water. He handed the bucket to Sun Child, and she drank and handed it back, and he drank as well, then refilled it. He gave it to her, pointing to her and then to the spring. She was to learn that it was her job to keep the house furnished with water.

Once back in the house, Cooper offered her some more of the brownish puffy mass he had given her on their journey, but she refused, remembering how ill it made her feel. He called it "bread." She repeated the word with a frown. She was hoping for a nice corn cake, but none was forthcoming, and she did not know how to ask for it.

Next she looked around for a pallet on which to sleep but saw none. She made a yawning motion and put her head to the side, closing her eyes. Cooper understood and pointed to the bedstead, saying the word "bed." Sun Child pointed to him and then the bed and repeated the word. Then she pointed to herself and made a questioning motion with her shoulders. He pointed at her and then at the bed.

The bed was at least as wide as the platform on which her parents had their pallet, but the thought of sleeping next to Cooper was not appealing to Sun Child. Nevertheless, she crawled onto it and rolled to the far side near the wall.

Cooper immediately pulled her out and began to remove her clothes. She pulled away from him, but he grabbed her again and continued. Once she was completely naked, he looked her up and down and turned her around, grinning from ear to ear. She did not like that grin. She jumped back into the bed, pulled the quilted cover over herself, and turned her face to the wall. She could hear that Cooper was doing something, but she didn't want to find out what it was.

Suddenly, she was aware that the lamp had gone out, and moments later, she felt the bed creak as Cooper got in. Sun Child stiffened, terrified of what she realized was coming next. Like all Indian girls her age, she knew about sex and was taught how wonderful it was between people who loved each other, but she also knew what rape was.

Cooper's hands were suddenly all over her, his mouth pressed on hers. She thought of her village and all that she had ever held dear and knew that it was lost to her forever with this disgusting act that was about to happen to her. She held her body as stiff as possible but knew that she was powerless to resist him. Fortunately, he ejaculated quickly and dropped off to sleep immediately. She lay there, weeping silently, until her own fatigue, both physical and emotional, was too much for her, and she fell asleep as well.

When she awoke in the morning, Cooper had a fire made on which he was cooking fish. As she threw back the bed covers and reached for her clothes that were lying on the floor, she saw that the bed and her legs were spotted with dried blood.

Thus began a life that was nothing short of hell for Sun Child. Far from being the queen Cooper had told her parents he would make her, she was basically his slave. She was made to keep house for him, to learn to cook like an Englishwoman, to sew his clothes and hers, to help with his goods, even to accompany him to other Indian villages and help him sell his wares. She often thought of running away, back to her village, but she didn't know where it was. Moreover, she knew that it would dishonor her parents. She knew they had had no idea what was in store for her, but they had given their word and had received goods for her. She saw no way out.

Stuart had been in Virginia for three years when his regiment traveled to the border of nearby Maryland to defend the settlers there against an invasion by the Iroquois. This tribe had been befriended by the Dutch, who had encouraged them to attack the Susquehannock, who were allies of the British. The British very much wanted the town the Dutch called New Amsterdam and its protective fort, Fort

Amsterdam. The Dutch, for their part, wanted the British out. The Dutch had been in the area for years and had established a lucrative trade of furs and fish. They had no intention of sharing that with the British.

Fortunately for the British, word of the proposed invasion got around, and British soldiers were waiting for the Iroquois when they attacked. Unfortunately for the British, the natives never followed the rules of warfare. They fought what would later be called a guerilla war, attacking as opportunity presented itself, hiding until ready, and picking off the British lines with their arrows as the British approached, regimental drums beating time and obscuring any noise that might otherwise provide warning.

By this point, Stuart had been through numerous battles with the natives and knew what to expect, but he was only a lieutenant, and his captain was fresh from England. Despite all warnings from every officer in the regiment, he insisted on using traditional British battle strategy.

Ultimately, the British and their Susquehannock allies were victorious, but their losses were many. First Stuart was hit in the thigh by an arrow; then his horse stumbled, and he was thrown to the ground and knocked unconscious when his head hit a rock. When he finally regained consciousness, the battle was over. All around him lay the bodies of the dead, both Indian and British. He guessed that the regiment had retreated to safer ground lest another wave of natives waited nearby.

The arrow was still in his leg, but the wound was clean and had stopped bleeding. He knew it would start again if he pulled the arrow out, and he might bleed to death, not to mention the pain that would cause, and it hurt enough already. He was able to stretch enough to reach a sapling that grew a few feet from his head. Using it, he was able to pull himself up, first to a sitting position and then to something more or less like standing.

He found a stick on the ground, and using it as a makeshift crutch, he stumbled toward the south, from which his regiment had come.

The sun was going down, and it was hard to find his way, but he knew his life depended on it. He was very hungry but saw nothing edible except a few hard blackberries left over from the summer, too hard for even the birds or bugs to eat but welcome to him just the same. He found a stream where he was able to drink and soak his throbbing leg, the dried blood floating away with the current. Then he pulled himself up and continued walking.

When night fell completely, he was exhausted. In the dark, he stumbled through a pile of leaves and twisted his good leg as it plunged into a hole filled with water. With great effort and in greater pain, he managed to extricate himself, but that was all he could do. He dropped down on the soft leaves and fell into a tortured, but nevertheless sound, sleep.

The sunlight shooting through the tree branches awakened him. He picked up his head and looked around, groggily trying to remember how he came to be where he was. When he tried to move further, it all came back, and he cried out aloud with pain. The leg with the arrow was completely stiff, and even his good leg ached from his fall. His mouth was dry, and he reached out to wet his hand in the dew and lick the moisture from it.

At that moment, he heard a rustling among the leaves and looked up to see a young woman approaching with a wooden bucket. She wore English clothes but no shoes or cap. At first he thought he was imagining her, but as she came closer, he saw that she was indeed real. Gathering up his courage, he spoke to her.

"Good morning!" he said as cheerfully as he could.

The girl jumped back, startled. Lost in her own thoughts, she had not seen him. She turned quickly and started to run away.

"Wait!" cried Stuart. "Come back! I'm wounded. Please help me!"

Slowly the girl turned around and looked at him. When she saw the arrow protruding from his leg, she obviously decided he could not harm her and warily made her way back to him.

"Please!" pleaded Stuart. "I don't know where I am or where my regiment is. Can you get someone to come and help me?"

"You are a soldier," said the girl. It was neither a statement nor a question, more as though she was trying to convince herself.

"Yes," said Stuart. "I was in a battle yesterday, and my regiment left me behind. They must have thought I was dead. Can you help me?"

The girl came closer and looked at his leg. "You have a bad hurt," she said. "I will help you."

She spoke her words very precisely and deliberately, as if she had not been speaking English for very long. The only people Stuart had known who spoke this way were natives who had just learned the language, but this girl was clearly not a native. Her English clothes, blue eyes, and curly hair belied any connection with natives. In addition, she was taller than any native woman he had ever seen.

"Come," she said.

"I would love to," said Stuart, "but I can't move."

"Yes, I will help you," she replied.

She took him by the hands and pulled him to a sitting position. She was amazingly strong for such a slender person. She knelt down and let him use her shoulder to push himself up; then she pulled his arm on the side of his hurt leg over her shoulders, letting her body be his crutch.

She led him to a tree and put his hand on the trunk so he could steady himself while she filled her bucket from the hole into which he had stepped, which he now realized was a spring. Then, holding her full bucket while supporting him, she slowly walked to the hill.

Although both of his legs screamed with pain, Stuart tried to make conversation with his benefactress, wanting her to feel comfortable with him.

"My name is Stuart Chapman," he said. "I'm a lieutenant in the Duke of York's regiment. My regiment came here from Fort Henry. What's your name?"

"My name is Martha Cooper," she said. "My husband is Francis Cooper. He is a trader."

"I know your husband!" Stuart said. "He has come to the fort to pick up goods and to sell pelts that he traded from the natives. Do you live nearby? Is your husband there? He will know where to get help for me."

"He is not there," said Martha. "He went to the big water to get more to trade. He will not help you. I will help you."

Stuart was confused. Either this woman was a native or she had lived among the natives. Sometimes natives took European children and raised them as their own. He was afraid to ask, though, afraid to insult her.

After a most painful climb up the hill, they reached Martha's house. She brought Stuart in and laid him on the bed. Then she went to a trunk and returned with a jug of liquid. She poured some into a cup and held it out to Stuart. "Drink," she said. She helped him to lift his shoulders so that he could do so.

Almost immediately, Stuart felt his pain dissipating. "What was that?" he asked, suddenly afraid she had poisoned him.

"Good medicine," she said. "You rest."

First she removed his boots and propped his leg up on pillows. Then she picked up a knife and cut away the pants leg around his wound. "I will take out arrow," she said in a matter-of-fact manner, as if doing so was something she did every day. First she swabbed the wound with a rag soaked in a brown liquid that smelled like fish. The liquid burned at first, but Stuart could tell it was meant to relieve the pain. Then she cut all around the wound. Stuart screamed in agony as the knife cut into his flesh, but in a few seconds she had the arrow out and had stanched the bleeding with the brown-liquid rag. Leaving him to hold the rag in place, she went back to the trunks that lined the wall and brought back a length of cloth, which she wrapped around and around his leg and tied off.

Stuart lay back in a cold sweat. His wound ached, and his head was swimming from the intense pain of the arrow removal. He wondered if maybe it would have been better if he had just died on the battlefield.

Soon he detected that there was fire nearby, and he began to smell something cooking. Shortly thereafter, Martha brought a cup of thick, steaming liquid and spooned it into his mouth. He had never tasted anything so good in all his life. With food and liquid in his system, he began to relax somewhat and finally fell asleep. He had many questions, but he felt too awful to ask them. They could wait.

As he slept, Martha kept watch, both to verify his condition and to keep a lookout for Cooper's return. She was not sure how Cooper would react to finding someone in his bed, but she reasoned that he should be happy that she had helped one of his people. She tried to figure out from looking at him what sort of person this soldier might be. He was younger and healthier than Cooper, for sure, and his skin was smooth, unlike Cooper's pockmarked body. His hair was the same brown color as Cooper's but thicker, and she had noticed that his eyes were brown. His features were regular and symmetrical. She had seen many soldiers during her trips to the forts with Cooper, and they had all looked pretty much the same to her. This one was different, and she didn't know why. She decided it must have been because he was in need and in pain. He had not looked at her with the disdain she had felt from other Englishmen.

When Stuart awakened, it was morning, the sun streaming in through the cabin's one window. Through sleep-fogged eyes, he could see Martha at the hearth, stirring something in a pot on the hob. He tried to turn over to see her better, but as he did, he twisted his wounded leg and cried out in pain.

Martha rushed over to him, and through the searing pain in his leg, he was again struck by her beauty. She helped him to sit up and fed him again, this time corn porridge flavored with smoked meat. It was delicious.

After breakfast, she encouraged him to try to get up and walk, saying it would keep his leg from getting too stiff. She was right. It felt good to him to move a little, and the proximity of her body as she served as his crutch was far from unpleasant.

By the end of a week, he was much, much better and could have left to return to his regiment, but he found he was loath to leave. On the one hand, he was afraid her husband would return, and he would have no reason for being there, since his wound was healing so well, but the more he got to know Martha, the more he liked her. She was quite accomplished for a woman of the wilderness. Cooper had taught her to read and write so that she could keep his accounts for him, and she also knew the ways of the forests, mountains, and fields. She was completely unconscious of the mores of "polite society" and thought nothing of changing her garments in front of him, yet he knew she was not trying to be seductive. Stuart found himself strongly attracted to her, but he kept his distance, both because she was another man's wife and because he respected her too much. Even though they slept in the same bed, he never touched her. He finally got the courage to ask about her upbringing, but she would not respond, and he didn't want to make her uncomfortable by prying.

For her part, she was disarmed by his gentleness. He helped her in every way he could and made no demands on her. In his eyes, she saw respect, something she had never experienced with Cooper. As their days together increased, she felt sexual desire for the first time in her life, but she didn't know what to do about it.

Finally, Stuart could delay no longer. He told her he would be leaving the following day. They walked together to the spring, Stuart carrying the full bucket up for her, and picked the first dewberries of the season, which Martha cooked with corn dumplings. Stuart had noticed that there was a sack of wheat flour in the cabin, but Martha never used it. When he had asked her why that was, she had said it made her sick. He had missed eating real bread, but he had not pressed her. After living on a soldier's rations for so long, he found her cooking to be wonderful.

As night fell, they lit the tallow lamp and sat down at the table for their last dinner together, a simple meal of boiled smoked venison and some kind of root that Martha had dug up in the woods. Stuart asked her what the root was called, but she said she didn't know, only that it was good to eat.

When bedtime came, Stuart shed all but his shirt and crawled into the bed. Martha began to disrobe as well, and whereas before, Stuart had averted his eyes when she did this, this time he let himself watch her, knowing it would be his last night with her. She had the kind of breasts that would one day be full, but she was still quite young, with her slender waist and almost boyish hips. As she raised her arms above her head to slip on her night shift, Stuart was almost overcome with desire. All he could do was turn his face to the wall and will himself calm.

Then she crawled in beside him and moved over to him, spooning his back, her arm over his shoulder. Stuart was startled when he felt her next to him but leaned into her body, wondering what to do next.

She decided that for him by running her hand down his leg. He turned toward her and kissed her gently. She responded by returning his kiss, but much more ardently. It was the permission he had hoped for.

Martha loved the gentle way he did everything, and he was delighted with her innocent lack of inhibition. Although he knew she was no novice to sex, she was very different from the camp followers with whom he had lain ever since he had joined the army.

When sleep became a necessity, they found it in each other's arms.

The next morning, they took their leave of each other, with the hope that they might see each other again even if they could never really be together again. "I know your name is Martha," Stuart said, "but for me, you will be Beatrice and I will be Dante. Maybe someday you will hear their story and remember me."

Part VII

Andrew became more and more manic as the weeks went by and his child by Lucy was not found. He began to hallucinate, believing that Lucy was there before him, chiding him because he had not tried harder to find her. He even went himself to his family estate, which he had heretofore managed through an employee, and questioned all the servants and other employees as to whether any of them had heard tales of the Digby family and where they had been taken. Either no one knew or no one was telling.

Andrew's health worsened. The ride on horseback to and from the Selden estate had been hard on him, and in typical Andrew fashion, he had not done it wisely, traveling rain or shine and pushing his horse unmercifully, only to leave him disappointed yet again.

Soon after returning to Chapman Hall, he began to cough, not the consumptive cough that had so weakened poor Basil, but the all-too-familiar cough of pneumonia. The doctor was called, and though leeching did remove some of the color from his feverish cheeks, it also weakened him. He was dead within a week.

Just before he died, a letter came from the Selden estate. It was from one of Oliver Boyle's sons, written for him by the curate. It explained that the man was afraid to speak to Andrew directly, afraid to be punished for not speaking up before, but he thought he remembered his father's having said that he had taken the Digbys to Eliot Manor, the home of one of Lord Selden's distant cousins in Lincolnshire.

Andrew never saw that letter. It lay unopened on his desk as he lay dying and was not discovered until two weeks after his burial when his lawyers came to sort out his papers.

Knowing that they could not execute Andrew's will and get their pay (the will specified that the estate was to pay no one until the provisions of the will were fulfilled) until they followed up on the letter, Robert Pearce, who had been named executor of Andrew's will, set off for Eliot Manor as soon as he could prepare himself.

During Andrew's illness, Pearce had contacted the elder

Chapmans, hoping for some clue regarding Andrew's oldest child. They knew nothing, and Stuart had already left for America, but they put him in touch with Benjamin. Benjamin was surprised to find that Andrew might have a living child but was not at all surprised that Stuart might receive everything by default, nor was he jealous, having found complete contentment in his religious vocation. He communicated his lack of knowledge to Pearce, asking Pearce to keep him informed, which Pearce promised to do.

Stuart had not long been back from his sojourn with Martha when Benjy's letter arrived. His feelings on hearing of Andrew's death and will ranged from sadness to anger to triumph to frustration to hope. On the one hand, he hated what Andrew had done to him and Benjy, but some part of him still loved Andrew and missed the closeness they had once shared. On the other, he saw that maybe, just maybe, he would be able to reclaim his estate, and gain even more, if no heir was found for Andrew. Since Andrew had acquired the Chapman estate through Judith, and Judith was Andrew's wife, her heir should be next in line, as was prescribed in Andrew's will. Benjy had laid all this out in the letter, having checked it with people who knew, and after communicating with Pearce, he was optimistic about no heir's being found. At the time he wrote to Stuart, however, Benjy was unaware of the letter from the Selden employee that had been found on Andrew's desk.

Stuart decided that it was time for him to act, so because he was still recovering from his wound and because no military actions seemed imminent, he was able to obtain permission to return to England on leave. Within a week of receiving Benjy's letter, he was on a ship bound for Southampton.

It took a month for Robert Pearce to arrange his life and work for a journey and to arrive at Eliot Manor. Sir David Eliot, its present owner, knew the Digbys, as some of the children still worked on the estate. His main mower, Edgar Webster, he said, had married one of the Digby grandchildren. Eventually Pearce found Emily Fletcher

Webster, Lucy's daughter by Peter Fletcher. She told Pearce that her parents and grandparents were all dead and that she had reason to believe that her only sibling, her brother Jeremy, was as well. She explained that Jeremy, who, as far as she knew, was the son of both of her parents, had probably died in America. When Pearce suggested that Jeremy might have had a different father, she said she guessed it was possible, since Jeremy didn't look like Peter Fletcher at all, and his personality was certainly different. He and Peter had quarreled all the time, she said, and it was their volatile relationship that had sent Jeremy into the army. Peter had wanted Jeremy to become a mower like himself and his grandfather Digby, but Jeremy always thought fieldwork was beneath his dignity and had gone off to the army as soon as he was old enough.

She showed Pearce the letter she had received from America telling of Jeremy's presumed death. She couldn't read it herself but had kept it as a memento. From the letter, Pearce was able to find out whom to contact.

By the time Stuart arrived in England and met with Pearce, Pearce had been able to find out that Jeremy's regiment was still in America. Stuart made no bones about his intentions, and Pearce was happy to have someone to do his legwork for him. Armed with the knowledge that his rival for Andrew's fortune was probably dead, Stuart returned to America to make sure of that. Stuart left for America well provided with names and locations and a detailed description of Jeremy that Pearce had obtained from Emily.

Whereas Stuart had mostly enjoyed his previous sea voyages, this one seemed interminable. He paced the deck irritably every day until the residual pain from his leg forced him to rest. He was so close! If he could provably determine that Andrew's son was dead, the Chapman estate was his again.

Once back on American soil, Stuart wasted no time locating Roger Walton, the present captain of the regiment of which Jeremy was once a member. Captain Johnson, he learned, had moved farther inland, and no one knew where he was. Walton was familiar with the story of the raid on the native village and its outcome. No Englishman had returned to the village to claim the English bodies, fearful of the natives' revenge, but it was assumed that anyone who had not returned was dead.

Presumption was not certainty and might not hold up in an English court. Stuart had to be certain before he could put forth any claims. He obtained from Walton the name and location of the village where the raid had taken place and set out. Knowing that, as an Englishman, he would also be in danger in that village, he disguised himself as a peddler, complete with a pack full of wares, and took with him a friend he had made early in his Virginia sojourn, a member the same tribal family who would be able to speak the language and vouch for him.

The natives received him and his escort respectfully but not warmly. Although they wanted the items the peddlers sold, and wanted to sell their goods, they had become aware that often they were being cheated.

In the course of his conversation with the village leaders, Stuart mentioned that he was looking for a man who had been his enemy in years past. When he described Jeremy, the leaders immediately sent for Sun Woman and her husband, who readily identified Jeremy as the person who had raped Sun Woman and whom her husband had killed.

When Stuart expressed delight that his enemy was dead, they punctured his bubble by telling him that a child had resulted from the rape. "Sun Child is her name," Sun Woman said, "and I miss her so much!"

"Miss her? Did she die, too?" Stuart asked through his translator, cautiously hopeful.

"Oh, I hope not," Sun Woman replied. "Her husband said she would be living in a fine house and would have everything she wanted."

"Husband?" Stuart asked. He knew enough about the natives

to know that usually, if a marriage took place between people of different villages, it was the man who went to live with the woman's clan, not the other way around. "Didn't she marry someone in the village?"

"No," said Sun Woman, tears coming to her eyes. She proceeded to tell Stuart what had happened with Sun Child, about how beautiful she was and what she looked like.

A lump had begun to form in Stuart's throat. "You say she married an English peddler. What was his name?"

Neither Sun Child nor her husband knew, but they called the woman who spoke English and who had helped to arrange the marriage.

"His name was Francis Cooper," the woman said.

Stuart went pale and almost fainted. His worst enemy was the woman he loved.

While Stuart was in England, life had changed drastically for Martha. About a week after Stuart left, Francis Cooper returned. After a couple of swigs from the rum barrel, as was his wont, he immediately checked on his possessions, including food, and found that more was missing than he thought Martha could have consumed alone.

When he questioned her, she did not lie.

"I found a soldier at the spring," she told him. "He was one of your people. He was badly wounded, so I helped him."

"How long did he stay here?" demanded Cooper.

"I don't know. Until he was well enough to walk back to his people."

"And you fed him the whole time? Did he pay you for the food he ate?"

"No. He was hurt. I thought it was right to help one of your countrymen."

"Well, you thought wrong. What else did you give him?"

"Just some clothes. His were ruined."

"How did they get ruined?"

"In a fight with the Iroquois. He had an arrow in his leg."

"You will never do that again, do you hear me?" Cooper yelled. "I work too hard for the food we have to find it squandered on some stranger! Now feed me. I'm your husband, the one who feeds you, you lazy savage!"

"Why do you speak to me like that? Haven't I always been a good wife?"

"You? A good wife? Let's see about that!"

With that he grabbed Martha and hauled her into the bed. He threw up her skirt and lost no time thrusting himself into her with as much force as possible.

His violence was such a contrast to Stuart's gentleness that Martha was enraged. Once he rolled off of her, she jumped from the bed and grabbed the poker from the fireplace.

"Don't ever touch me again!" she cried. "I want to go home to my people. I hate you!"

"Oh, our little half-breed has a temper! Your people don't want you, you whore. If it weren't for me, you'd be married to some old man in your village, pretending to have sex with a dead member."

"No. I would live alone. I know how to take care of myself."

"You little shrew. I'll rip you to shreds!"

With that, he grabbed at her, but she was too quick for him. She poked him in the eye with the poker, and as he screamed in pain, she began beating him with it. The hard labor she had had to do had strengthened her, and her passion lent her extra strength. With the beating, the pain in his eye, and the rum he had consumed, he was no match for her. He stumbled and fell, and she seized a large log from the fire box and bludgeoned him with it until he lay still.

At that point, she began to panic. Not knowing what else to do, she took the fireplace shovel and spread embers all around the cabin, inside and out, then threw straw from the mule's pen over the embers. Soon the cabin was ablaze. She watched it for a few minutes and then fled. She had no idea where she was going, just that she wanted to get as far away as possible.

She ran into the woods and kept on running until her lungs felt as though they would burst, then sat down under a tree and tried to get her bearings. By the sun, she still had a few hours before sundown. The sun was to her left, so she walked straight ahead. Several times she had gone with her husband to a fort north of the cabin. She hoped someone there would take pity on her and help her to get back to her people. She had no idea whether her people would accept her, but they were all she had.

After two more hours, she arrived at the fort. She realized that it must have been the one from which Stuart and his fellow soldiers had come when they were ambushed by the Iroquois.

The last time she was at that fort, she had made friends with a French woman who had been captured by the English much farther north and had been brought south because she was a skilled herbalist. It was that woman who had taught her about the medicines she had used to help Stuart. It did not take her long to find this woman, Madame Denise, as she was called. The French woman welcomed her and told her she could stay with her as her assistant, at least for the time being.

Stuart had left the Indian village in shock. It appeared that the person he called Martha was really Sun Child, Andrew's granddaughter and heir to all of Andrew's property. Everything in his being told him that this couldn't be so, and yet, apparently, it was.

He had to find her. He set out immediately for the cabin where he had stayed with her.

It took some time for him to find it. He followed the path he remembered taking just before the ambush, and he actually found the battle site, which still had some grisly remnants of the battle. He tried to remember how he had found the spring where Martha had found him, but he had been in too much pain, and it had been too dark.

Finally, after getting lost and retracing his steps numerous times, he found the spring. It was covered with leaves and looked as though no one had used it in a long time. That boded ill, but he continued up the hill, as he had many times while carrying water for Martha.

His heart sank when he saw the cabin. Nothing was left but cinders, it seemed. He went and poked among them, discovering as he did so what appeared to be human bones. He was glad that the bones looked too long to be those of a woman. There was still hope.

Where could she have gone, if indeed she was still alive? What had happened? Who had died there?

So many questions swirled through his head as he made his way to the fort from which his troop had ridden not long before they were attacked.

Approaching the fort, he put on his army uniform so that no one would question his presence. Once inside, he was ushered into the quarters of the commander of the fort, Col. Hardy. He asked if anyone knew anything about Francis Cooper, the peddler. The commander said he had been wondering about Francis but hadn't seen him for awhile.

"His wife says he's up north getting supplies, but I wish he would hurry," said the commander. "My men have needs that he usually is able to meet, but he's way past due."

"His wife? You know where his wife is?" Stuart cried.

"Yes," said the commander. "She's been here for the last two weeks. That French woman who takes care of our sick men has been looking after her. Nice looking girl. Half savage, I think."

Stuart tried to look composed.

"Where is she? May I see her? I think she has something that belongs to me."

"Oh, really? Did she swipe something while old Cooper was trying to talk you into buying something you didn't need?" asked the commander, laughing.

"You might say that," said Stuart, trying to sound calm.

"Well, that French woman lives up against the east palisade.

You should find her there. You'll see the herb garden just beside her quarters."

"Thanks," said Stuart, starting to tremble.

A few strides and he was there. He called her name, but there was no answer. Then he saw her. She was bending over some plant in the garden, dressed like a peasant woman, with a muslin field bonnet on her head. He could see her dark braids, the ends curling beneath the brim of the bonnet. He could picture her bare feet, her toes gripping the dirt between the rows of plants.

"Martha!" he called again.

This time she heard him. She stood up abruptly but didn't turn toward him at first. Then, ever so slowly, he saw her head rotate in his direction. A smile lit up her face, and suddenly she was in his arms.

They had much to discuss, but first they needed time just to be together.

When they were finally able to pull apart from each other, Stuart waited before telling her his news. He wanted to hear what had happened at the cabin.

She swore him to secrecy but told him the truth. He told her that she shouldn't worry, that he didn't blame her for what she had done, and that there was little chance that anyone would even question the situation. Even if they found the cabin and the bones, Cooper's drinking was well known, and the few people who even knew that he lived in that cabin would assume that he had set it afire in a drunken stupor while his wife was at the fort and knew nothing about it.

Finally, he told her the story of her family and his. She couldn't believe it. He assured her that it was so and explained all he had found out from Pearce.

"But what will we do?" she asked. "I don't want all those things. I wouldn't know what to do with them. Besides, they really belong to you."

"No, my love, my Beatrice, they belong to us," Stuart said, taking her in his arms, "and we are going to England to claim them."

Just going to England wasn't enough, of course, as Stuart well knew. After extensive correspondence with Pearce, Stuart made sure they left America armed with certified affidavits from the captain of Jeremy's former company, Martha's parents, and everyone else Stuart could find who knew anything of the situation. Martha was delighted to see her parents again, even though they had essentially sold her into slavery, and Sun Woman wept with joy when she saw her daughter. Martha knew her parents had been duped by Cooper and did not hold them responsible for the horrible life she had led with him. She also knew she could never return to her village, though; she had resigned herself to that shortly after she left with Cooper, and her visit to the village with Stuart only confirmed it. It was no longer her home. Life had changed so much for her that crossing the ocean with Stuart did not frighten her.

Pearce met them in London, and they signed the papers that gave them possession of all of Andrew's possessions and paid Pearce and his colleagues for their work on Andrew's behalf.

Their next stop was Chapman Hall, where Benjy was waiting for them and where he officiated at their wedding at the village church. Sophia and Sir William were able to attend, as was Diana. Sir Henry's arthritis had worsened even more, so he was unable to make the journey. All three grandparents in attendance were beside themselves with happiness in seeing the good fortune of their grandson and meeting his bride, whose sweet nature endeared her to them immediately. Geoff and Sally stood as matron of honor and best man, and Clara and Colin stood as honorary matron of honor and best man for the couple.

As sort of a honeymoon, Stuart and Beatrice, as he now insisted on calling Sun Child, went first to the Selden estate so that Beatrice could see where her grandparents were raised, and then to Eliot Manor so that she could meet her Aunt Emily, who wept with joy to find that some part of the brother whom she had loved so much had survived. No one told her how he came to be Beatrice's father.

Before he left Virginia, Stuart had set in motion the process getting himself discharged from the army, and soon he received the paperwork required for completion. He was not sorry. The reality of war had not proven to be the glorious and exciting experience he had thought he wanted. Like Richard before him, he was looking forward to settling into the life of a country gentleman.

Before that could happen, however, he and Beatrice chose to divest themselves of all of Andrew's properties other than those that were their birthrights through the Seldens and the Chapmans. In every case where they were able, they sold the property, at a greatly discounted price, to the family who had lost it to Andrew. Since the Restoration, the fortunes of the gentry had improved, and through Stuart and Beatrice's generosity, numerous families were able to return to the estates of their ancestors. One of the beneficiaries of this process was his own Aunt Sally, who had been struggling to hang onto Alex's family estate while still paying Andrew's estate what Alex owed him, and was about to remarry when Stuart and Beatrice arrived in England. Geoff and Stephen, of course, also had their debts cancelled.

Stuart and Beatrice put the money that they made from selling the properties into investments for the future and for any children that they might have, but they also settled a nice sum on Benjy and prevailed upon the elder Chapmans to leave Benjy their small estate when they died. Benjy, who had never cared about money, was nevertheless delighted that he would have the resources to acquire the position he desired on completion of his theological studies. Emily Fletcher Webster was very surprised, too, when Pearce arrived to tell her that her niece had sent her a present of more money than she had expected to have all of her life.

Traveling around the country taking care of the property sales gave Stuart the chance to show Beatrice his country, many parts of which he had never seen himself. Beatrice loved the forests best, as they reminded her of her Virginia home.

Stuart put to good use the information about farming that he had learned while a youth at Chapman Hall and from the natives in Virginia. The wheat farming on the Selden estate was new to him, but he learned quickly. He kept on all the employees on the two estates and trusted them when he and Beatrice were away, which was often, since they had both to care for. Both the Chapman and the Selden estates became more productive than ever under his care.

For her part, Beatrice was overwhelmed by the grandeur in which she lived and sent a letter to her parents telling them that Cooper's promise to her had finally come to pass: she was truly living like a queen in a palace.

To contact the author:

Email: fontenotlandry@yahoo.com
Website: juliefontenotlandry.com

Made in the USA
San Bernardino, CA
06 May 2017